The Experiences of Loveday Brooke, Lady Detective

The Experiences of Loveday Brooke, Lady Detective

Catherine Louisa Pirkis

MINT EDITIONS

The Experiences of Loveday Brooke, Lady Detective was first published in 1893.

This edition published by Mint Editions 2021.

ISBN 9781513271989 | E-ISBN 9781513276984

Published by Mint Editions®

 MINT
EDITIONS

minteditionbooks.com

Publishing Director: Jennifer Newens
Design & Production: Rachel Lopez Metzger
Project Manager: Micaela Clark
Typesetting: Westchester Publishing Services

Contents

The Black Bag Left on a Door-Step

I t's a big thing," said Loveday Brooke, addressing Ebenezer Dyer, chief of the well-known detective agency in Lynch Court, Fleet Street; "Lady Cathrow has lost £30,000 worth of jewellery, if the newspaper accounts are to be trusted."

"They are fairly accurate this time. The robbery differs in few respects from the usual run of country-house robberies. The time chosen, of course, was the dinner-hour, when the family and guests were at table and the servants not on duty were amusing themselves in their own quarters. The fact of its being Christmas Eve would also of necessity add to the business and consequent distraction of the household. The entry to the house, however, in this case was not effected in the usual manner by a ladder to the dressing-room window, but through the window of a room on the ground floor—a small room with one window and two doors, one of which opens into the hall, and the other into a passage that leads by the back stairs to the bedroom floor. It is used, I believe, as a sort of hat and coat room by the gentlemen of the house."

"It was, I suppose, the weak point of the house?"

"Quite so. A very weak point indeed. Craigen Court, the residence of Sir George and Lady Cathrow, is an oddly-built old place, jutting out in all directions, and as this window looked out upon a blank wall, it was filled in with stained glass, kept fastened by a strong brass catch, and never opened, day or night, ventilation being obtained by means of a glass ventilator fitted in the upper panes. It seems absurd to think that this window, being only about four feet from the ground, should have had neither iron bars nor shutters added to it; such, however, was the case. On the night of the robbery, someone within the house must have deliberately, and of intention, unfastened its only protection, the brass catch, and thus given the thieves easy entrance to the house."

"Your suspicions, I suppose, centre upon the servants?"

"Undoubtedly; and it is in the servants' hall that your services will be required. The thieves, whoever they were, were perfectly cognizant of the ways of the house. Lady Cathrow's jewellery was kept in a safe in her dressing-room, and as the dressing-room was over the dining-room, Sir George was in the habit of saying that it was the 'safest' room in the house. (Note the pun, please; Sir George is rather proud of it.) By his orders the window of the dining-room immediately under the dressing-room window was always left unshuttered and without blind during dinner, and as a full stream of light thus fell through it on to the outside terrace, it would have been impossible for anyone to have placed a ladder there unseen."

"I see from the newspapers that it was Sir George's invariable custom to fill his house and give a large dinner on Christmas Eve."

"Yes. Sir George and Lady Cathrow are elderly people, with no family and few relatives, and have consequently a large amount of time to spend on their friends."

"I suppose the key of the safe was frequently left in the possession of Lady Cathrow's maid?"

"Yes. She is a young French girl, Stephanie Delcroix by name. It was her duty to clear the dressing-room directly after her mistress left it; put away any jewellery that might be lying about, lock the safe, and keep the key till her mistress came up to bed. On the night of the robbery, however, she admits that, instead of so doing, directly her mistress left the dressing-room, she ran down to the housekeeper's room to see if any letters had come for her, and remained chatting with the other servants for some time—she could not say for how long. It was by the half-past-seven post that her letters generally arrived from St. Omer, where her home is."

"Oh, then, she was in the habit of thus running down to enquire for her letters, no doubt, and the thieves, who appear to be so thoroughly cognizant of the house, would know this also."

"Perhaps; though at the present moment I must say things look very black against the girl. Her manner, too, when questioned, is not calculated to remove suspicion. She goes from one fit of hysterics into another; contradicts herself nearly every time she opens her mouth, then lays it to the charge of her ignorance of our language; breaks into voluble French; becomes theatrical in action, and then goes off into hysterics once more."

"All that is quite Français, you know," said Loveday. "Do the authorities at Scotland Yard lay much stress on the safe being left unlocked that night?"

"They do, and they are instituting a keen enquiry as to the possible lovers the girl may have. For this purpose they have sent Bates down to stay in the village and collect all the information he can outside the house. But they want someone within the walls to hob-nob with the maids generally, and to find out if she has taken any of them into her confidence respecting her lovers. So they sent to me to know if I would send down for this purpose one of the shrewdest and most clear-headed of my female detectives. I, in my turn, Miss Brooke, have sent for you—you may take it as a compliment if you like. So please now get out your note-book, and I'll give you sailing orders."

Loveday Brooke, at this period of her career, was a little over thirty years of age, and could be best described in a series of negations.

She was not tall, she was not short; she was not dark, she was not fair; she was neither handsome nor ugly. Her features were altogether nondescript; her one noticeable trait was a habit she had, when absorbed in thought, of dropping her eyelids over her eyes till only a line of eyeball showed, and she appeared to be looking out at the world through a slit, instead of through a window.

Her dress was invariably black, and was almost Quaker-like in its neat primness.

Some five or six years previously, by a jerk of Fortune's wheel, Loveday had been thrown upon the world penniless and all but friendless. Marketable accomplishments she had found she had none, so she had forthwith defied convention, and had chosen for herself a career that had cut her off sharply from her former associates and her position in society. For five or six years she drudged away patiently in the lower walks of her profession; then chance, or, to speak more precisely, an intricate criminal case, threw her in the way of the experienced head of the flourishing detective agency in Lynch Court. He quickly enough found out the stuff she was made of, and threw her in the way of better-class work—work, indeed, that brought increase of pay and of reputation alike to him and to Loveday.

Ebenezer Dyer was not, as a rule, given to enthusiasm; but he would at times wax eloquent over Miss Brooke's qualifications for the profession she had chosen.

"Too much of a lady, do you say?" he would say to anyone who chanced to call in question those qualifications. "I don't care twopence-halfpenny whether she is or is not a lady. I only know she is the most sensible and practical woman I ever met. In the first place, she has the faculty—so rare among women—of carrying out orders to the very letter: in the second place, she has a clear, shrewd brain, unhampered by any hard-and-fast theories; thirdly, and most important item of all, she has so much common sense that it amounts to genius—positively to genius, sir."

But although Loveday and her chief as a rule, worked together upon an easy and friendly footing, there were occasions on which they were wont, so to speak, to snarl at each other.

Such an occasion was at hand now.

Loveday showed no disposition to take out her note-book and receive her "sailing orders."

"I want to know," she said, "If what I saw in one newspaper is true—that one of the thieves before leaving, took the trouble to close the safe-door, and to write across it in chalk: 'To be let, unfurnished'?"

"Perfectly true; but I do not see that stress need be laid on the fact. The scoundrels often do that sort of thing out of insolence or bravado. In that robbery at Reigate, the other day, they went to a lady's Davenport, took a sheet of her note-paper, and wrote their thanks on it for her kindness in not having had the lock of her safe repaired. Now, if you will get out your note-book—"

"Don't be in such a hurry," said Loveday calmly: "I want to know if you have seen this?" She leaned across the writing-table at which they sat, one either side, and handed to him a newspaper cutting which she took from her letter-case.

Mr. Dyer was a tall, powerfully-built man with a large head, benevolent bald forehead and a genial smile. That smile, however, often proved a trap to the unwary, for he owned a temper so irritable that a child with a chance word might ruffle it.

The genial smile vanished as he took the newspaper cutting from Loveday's hand.

"I would have you to remember, Miss Brooke," he said severely, "that although I am in the habit of using dispatch in my business, I am never known to be in a hurry; hurry in affairs I take to be the especial mark of the slovenly and unpunctual."

Then, as if still further to give contradiction to her words, he very deliberately unfolded her slip of newspaper and slowly, accentuating each word and syllable, read as follows:—

"A black leather bag, or portmanteau, was found early yesterday morning by one of Smith's newspaper boys on the doorstep of a house in the road running between Easterbrook and Wreford, and inhabited by an elderly spinster lady. The contents of the bag include a clerical collar and necktie, a Church Service, a book of sermons, a copy of the works of Virgil, a *facsimile* of Magna Charta, with translations, a pair of black kid gloves, a brush and comb, some newspapers, and several small articles suggesting clerical ownership. On the top of the bag the following extraordinary letter, written in pencil on a long slip of paper, was found:

'The fatal day has arrived. I can exist no longer. I go hence and shall be no more seen. But I would have Coroner and Jury know that I am a sane man, and a verdict of temporary insanity in my case would be an error most gross after this intimation. I care not if it is *felo de se*, as I shall have passed all suffering. Search diligently for my poor lifeless body in the immediate neighbourhood—on the cold heath, the rail, or the river by yonder bridge—a few moments will decide how I shall depart. If I had walked aright I might have been a power in the Church of which I am now an unworthy member and priest; but the damnable sin of gambling got hold on me, and betting has been my ruin, as it has been the ruin of thousands who have preceded me. Young man, shun the bookmaker and the race-course as you would shun the devil and hell. Farewell, chums of Magdalen. Farewell, and take warning. Though I can claim relationship with a Duke, a Marquess, and a Bishop, and though I am the son of a noble woman, yet am I a tramp and an outcast, verily and indeed. Sweet death, I greet thee. I dare not sign my name. To one and all, farewell. O, my poor Marchioness mother, a dying kiss to thee. R.I.P.'

"The police and some of the railway officials have made a 'diligent search' in the neighbourhood of the railway station, but no 'poor lifeless body' has been found. The police authorities are inclined to the belief that the letter is a hoax, though they are still investigating the matter."

In the same deliberate fashion as he had opened and read the cutting, Mr. Dyer folded and returned it to Loveday.

"May I ask," he said sarcastically, "what you see in that silly hoax to waste your and my valuable time over?"

"I wanted to know," said Loveday, in the same level tones as before, "if you saw anything in it that might in some way connect this discovery with the robbery at Craigen Court?"

Mr. Dyer stared at her in utter, blank astonishment.

"When I was a boy," he said sarcastically as before, "I used to play at a game called 'what is my thought like?' Someone would think of something absurd—say the top of the monument—and someone else would hazard a guess that his thought might be—say the toe of his left boot, and that unfortunate individual would have to show the connection between the toe of his left boot and the top of the monument. Miss Brooke, I have no wish to repeat the silly game this evening for your benefit and mine."

"Oh, very well," said Loveday, calmly; "I fancied you might like to talk it over, that was all. Give me my 'sailing orders,' as you call them, and I'll endeavour to concentrate my attention on the little French maid and her various lovers."

Mr. Dyer grew amiable again.

"That's the point on which I wish you to fix your thoughts," he said; "you had better start for Craigen Court by the first train to-morrow—it's about sixty miles down the Great Eastern line. Huxwell is the station you must land at. There one of the grooms from the Court will meet you, and drive you to the house. I have arranged with the housekeeper there— Mrs. Williams, a very worthy and discreet person—that you shall pass in the house for a niece of hers, on a visit to recruit, after severe study in order to pass board-school teachers' exams. Naturally you have injured your eyes as well as your health with overwork; and so you can wear your blue spectacles. Your name, by the way, will be Jane Smith—better write it down. All your work will be among the servants of the establishment, and there will be no necessity for you to see either Sir George or Lady Cathrow—in fact, neither of them have been apprised of your intended visit—the fewer we take into our confidence the better. I've no doubt, however, that Bates will hear from Scotland Yard that you are in the house, and will make a point of seeing you."

"Has Bates unearthed anything of importance?"

"Not as yet. He has discovered one of the girl's lovers, a young farmer of the name of Holt; but as he seems to be an honest, respectable young fellow, and entirely above suspicion, the discovery does not count for much."

"I think there's nothing else to ask," said Loveday, rising to take her departure. "Of course, I'll telegraph, should need arise, in our usual cipher."

The first train that left Bishopsgate for Huxwell on the following morning included, among its passengers, Loveday Brooke, dressed in the neat black supposed to be appropriate to servants of the upper class. The only literature with which she had provided herself in order to beguile the tedium of her journey was a small volume bound in paper boards, and entitled, "The Reciter's Treasury." It was published at the low price of one shilling, and seemed specially designed to meet the requirements of third-rate amateur reciters at penny readings.

Miss Brooke appeared to be all-absorbed in the contents of this book during the first half of her journey. During the second, she lay back in the carriage with closed eyes, and motionless as if asleep or lost in deep thought.

The stopping of the train at Huxwell aroused her, and set her collecting together her wraps.

It was easy to single out the trim groom from Craigen Court from among the country loafers on the platform. Someone else beside the trim groom at the same moment caught her eye—Bates, from Scotland Yard, got up in the style of a commercial traveler, and carrying the orthodox "commercial bag" in his hand. He was a small, wiry man, with red hair and whiskers, and an eager, hungry expression of countenance.

"I am half-frozen with cold," said Loveday, addressing Sir George's groom; "if you'll kindly take charge of my portmanteau, I'd prefer walking to driving to the Court."

The man gave her a few directions as to the road she was to follow, and then drove off with her box, leaving her free to indulge Mr. Bate's evident wish for a walk and confidential talk along the country road.

Bates seemed to be in a happy frame of mind that morning.

"Quite a simple affair, this, Miss Brooke," he said: "a walk over the course, I take it, with you working inside the castle walls and I unearthing without. No complications as yet have arisen, and if that girl does not find herself in jail before another week is over her head, my name is not Jeremiah Bates."

"You mean the French maid?"

"Why, yes, of course. I take it there's little doubt but what she performed the double duty of unlocking the safe and the window too. You see I look at it this way, Miss Brooke: all girls have lovers, I say to myself, but a pretty girl like that French maid, is bound to have double the number of lovers than the plain ones. Now, of course, the greater the number of lovers, the greater the chance there is of a criminal being found among them. That's plain as a pikestaff, isn't it?"

"Just as plain."

Bates felt encouraged to proceed.

"Well, then, arguing on the same lines, I say to myself, this girl is only a pretty, silly thing, not an accomplished criminal, or she wouldn't have admitted leaving open the safe door; give her rope enough and she'll hang herself. In a day or two, if we let her alone, she'll be bolting off to join the fellow whose nest she has helped to feather, and we shall catch the pair of them 'twixt here and Dover Straits, and also possibly get a clue that will bring us on the traces of their accomplices. Eh, Miss Brooke, that'll be a thing worth doing?"

"Undoubtedly. Who is this coming along in this buggy at such a good pace?"

The question was added as the sound of wheels behind them made her look round.

Bates turned also. "Oh, this is young Holt; his father farms land about a couple of miles from here. He is one of Stephanie's lovers, and I should imagine about the best of the lot. But he does not appear to be first favourite; from what I hear someone else must have made the running on the sly. Ever since the robbery I'm told the young woman has given him the cold shoulder."

As the young man came nearer in his buggy he slackened pace, and Loveday could not but admire his frank, honest expression of countenance,

"Room for one—can I give you a lift?" he said, as he came alongside of them.

And to the ineffable disgust of Bates, who had counted upon at least an hour's confidential talk with her, Miss Brooke accepted the young farmer's offer, and mounted beside him in his buggy.

As they went swiftly along the country road, Loveday explained to the young man that her destination was Craigen Court, and that as she was a stranger to the place, she must trust to him to put her down at the nearest point to it that he would pass.

At the mention of Craigen Court his face clouded.

"They're in trouble there, and their trouble has brought trouble on others," he said a little bitterly.

"I know," said Loveday sympathetically; "it is often so. In such circumstances as these suspicions frequently fastens on an entirely innocent person."

"That's it! that's it!" he cried excitedly; "if you go into that house you'll hear all sorts of wicked things said of her, and see everything setting in dead against her. But she's innocent. I swear to you she is as innocent as you or I are."

His voice rang out above the clatter of his horse's hoots. He seemed to forget that he had mentioned no name, and that Loveday, as a stranger, might be at a loss to know to whom he referred.

"Who is guilty Heaven only knows," he went on after a moment's pause; "it isn't for me to give an ill name to anyone in that house; but I only say she is innocent, and that I'll stake my life on."

"She is a lucky girl to have found one to believe in her, and trust her as you do," said Loveday, even more sympathetically than before.

"Is she? I wish she'd take advantage of her luck, then," he answered bitterly. "Most girls in her position would be glad to have a man to stand by them through thick and thin. But not she! Ever since the night of that accursed robbery she has refused to see me—won't answer my letters—won't even send me a message. And, great Heavens! I'd marry her to-morrow, if I had the chance, and dare the world to say a word against her."

He whipped up his pony. The hedges seemed to fly on either side of them, and before Loveday realized that half her drive was over, he had drawn rein, and was helping her to alight at the servants' entrance to Craigen Court.

"You'll tell her what I've said to you, if you get the opportunity, and beg her to see me, if only for five minutes?" he petitioned before he re-mounted his buggy. And Loveday, as she thanked the young man for his kind attention, promised to make an opportunity to give his message to the girl.

Mrs. Williams, the housekeeper, welcomed Loveday in the servants' hall, and then took her to her own room to pull off her wraps. Mrs. Williams was the widow of a London tradesman, and a little beyond the average housekeeper in speech and manner.

She was a genial, pleasant woman, and readily entered into conversation with Loveday. Tea was brought in, and each seemed to feel at home with the other. Loveday in the course of this easy, pleasant talk, elicited from her the whole history of the events of the day of the robbery, the number and names of the guests who sat down to dinner that night, together with some other apparently trivial details.

The housekeeper made no attempt to disguise the painful position in which she and every one of the servants of the house felt themselves to be at the present moment.

"We are none of us at our ease with each other now," she said, as she poured out hot tea for Loveday, and piled up a blazing fire. "Everyone fancies that everyone else is suspecting him or her, and trying to rake up past words or deeds to bring in as evidence. The whole house seems under a cloud. And at this time of year, too; just when everything as a rule is at its merriest!" and here she gave a doleful glance to the big bunch of holly and mistletoe hanging from the ceiling.

"I suppose you are generally very merry downstairs at Christmas time?" said Loveday. "Servants' balls, theatricals, and all that sort of thing?"

"I should think we were! When I think of this time last year and the fun we all had, I can scarcely believe it is the same house. Our ball always follows my lady's ball, and we have permission to ask our friends to it, and we keep it up as late as ever we please. We begin our evening with a concert and recitations in character, then we have a supper and then we dance right on till morning; but this year!"—she broke off, giving a long, melancholy shake of her head that spoke volumes.

"I suppose," said Loveday, "some of your friends are very clever as musicians or reciters?"

"Very clever indeed. Sir George and my lady are always present during the early part of the evening, and I should like you to have seen Sir George last year laughing fit to kill himself at Harry Emmett dressed in prison dress with a bit of oakum in his hand, reciting the "Noble Convict!" Sir George said if the young man had gone on the stage, he would have been bound to make his fortune."

"Half a cup, please," said Loveday, presenting her cup. "Who was this Harry Emmett then—a sweetheart of one of the maids?"

"Oh, he would flirt with them all, but he was sweetheart to none. He was footman to Colonel James, who is a great friend of Sir George's, and Harry was constantly backwards and forwards bringing messages from his master. His father, I think, drove a cab in London, and Harry for a time did so also; then he took it into his head to be a gentleman's servant, and great satisfaction he gave as such. He was always such a bright, handsome young fellow and so full of fun, that everyone liked him. But I shall tire you with all this; and you, of course, want to talk about something so different;" and the housekeeper sighed again, as the thought of the dreadful robbery entered her brain once more.

"Not at all. I am greatly interested in you and your festivities. Is Emmett still in the neighbourhood? I should amazingly like to hear him recite myself."

"I'm sorry to say he left Colonel James about six months ago. We all missed him very much at first. He was a good, kind-hearted young man, and I remember he told me he was going away to look after his dear old grandmother, who had a sweet-stuff shop somewhere or other, but where I can't remember."

Loveday was leaning back in her chair now, with eyelids drooped so low that she literally looked out through "slits" instead of eyes.

CATHERINE LOUISA PIRKIS

Suddenly and abruptly she changed the conversation.

"When will it be convenient for me to see Lady Cathrow's dressing-room?" she asked.

The housekeeper looked at her watch. "Now, at once," she answered: "it's a quarter to five now and my lady sometimes goes up to her room to rest for half an hour before she dresses for dinner."

"Is Stephanie still in attendance on Lady Cathrow?" Miss Brooke asked as she followed the housekeeper up the back stairs to the bedroom floor.

"Yes, Sir George and my lady have been goodness itself to us through this trying time, and they say we are all innocent till we are proved guilty, and will have it that none of our duties are to be in any way altered."

"Stephanie is scarcely fit to perform hers, I should imagine?"

"Scarcely. She was in hysterics nearly from morning till night for the first two or three days after the detectives came down, but now she has grown sullen, eats nothing and never speaks a word to any of us except when she is obliged. This is my lady's dressing-room, walk in please."

Loveday entered a large, luxuriously furnished room, and naturally made her way straight to the chief point of attraction in it—the iron safe fitted into the wall that separated the dressing-room from the bedroom.

It was a safe of the ordinary description, fitted with a strong iron door and Chubb lock. And across this door was written with chalk in characters that seemed defiant in their size and boldness, the words: "To be let, unfurnished."

LOVEDAY SPENT ABOUT FIVE MINUTES in front of this safe, all her attention concentrated upon the big, bold writing.

She took from her pocket-book a narrow strip of tracing-paper and compared the writing on it, letter by letter, with that on the safe door. This done she turned to Mrs. Williams and professed herself ready to follow her to the room below.

Mrs. Williams looked surprised. Her opinion of Miss Brooke's professional capabilities suffered considerable diminution.

"The gentlemen detectives," she said, "spent over an hour in this room; they paced the floor, they measured the candles, they—"

"Mrs. Williams," interrupted Loveday, "I am quite ready to look at the room below." Her manner had changed from gossiping friendliness to that of the business woman hard at work at her profession.

Without another word, Mrs. Williams led the way to the little room which had proved itself to be the "weak point" of the house.

They entered it by the door which opened into a passage leading to the back-stairs of the house. Loveday found the room exactly what it had been described to her by Mr. Dyer. It needed no second glance at the window to see the ease with which anyone could open it from the outside, and swing themselves into the room, when once the brass catch had been unfastened.

Loveday wasted no time here. In fact, much to Mrs. Williams's surprise and disappointment, she merely walked across the room, in at one door and out at the opposite one, which opened into the large inner hall of the house.

Here, however, she paused to ask a question:

"Is that chair always placed exactly in that position?" she said, pointing to an oak chair that stood immediately outside the room they had just quitted.

The housekeeper answered in the affirmative. It was a warm corner. "My lady" was particular that everyone who came to the house on messages should have a comfortable place to wait in.

"I shall be glad if you will show me to my room now," said Loveday, a little abruptly; "and will you kindly send up to me a county trade directory, if, that is, you have such a thing in the house?"

Mrs. Williams, with an air of offended dignity, led the way to the bedroom quarters once more. The worthy housekeeper felt as if her own dignity had, in some sort, been injured by the want of interest Miss Brooke had evinced in the rooms which, at the present moment, she considered the "show" rooms of the house.

"Shall I send someone to help you unpack?" she asked, a little stiffly, at the door of Loveday's room.

"No, thank you; there will not be much unpacking to do. I must leave here by the first up-train to-morrow morning."

"To-morrow morning! Why, I have told everyone you will be here at least a fortnight!"

"Ah, then you must explain that I have been suddenly summoned home by telegram. I'm sure I can trust you to make excuses for me. Do not, however, make them before supper-time. I shall like to sit down to that meal with you. I suppose I shall see Stephanie then?"

The housekeeper answered in the affirmative, and went her way, wondering over the strange manners of the lady whom, at first, she had been disposed to consider "such a nice, pleasant, conversable person!"

At supper-time, however, when the upper-servants assembled at what was, to them, the pleasantest meal of the day, a great surprise was to greet them.

Stephanie did not take her usual place at table, and a fellow-servant, sent to her room to summon her returned, saying that the room was empty, and Stephanie was nowhere to be found.

Loveday and Mrs. Williams together went to the girl's bed-room. It bore its usual appearance: no packing had been done in it, and, beyond her hat and jacket, the girl appeared to have taken nothing away with her.

On enquiry, it transpired that Stephanie had, as usual, assisted Lady Cathrow to dress for dinner; but after that not a soul in the house appeared to have seen her.

Mrs. Williams thought the matter of sufficient importance to be at once reported to her master and mistress; and Sir George, in his turn, promptly dispatched a messenger to Mr. Bates, at the "King's Head," to summon him to an immediate consultation.

Loveday dispatched a messenger in another direction—to young Mr. Holt, at his farm, giving him particulars of the girl's disappearance.

Mr. Bates had a brief interview with Sir George in his study, from which he emerged radiant. He made a point of seeing Loveday before he left the Court, sending a special request to her that she would speak to him for a minute in the outside drive.

Loveday put her hat on, and went out to him. She found him almost dancing for glee.

"Told you so! told you so! Now, didn't I, Miss Brooke?" he exclaimed. "We'll come upon her traces before morning, never fear. I'm quite prepared. I knew what was in her mind all along. I said to myself, when that girl bolts it will be after she has dressed my lady for dinner—when she has two good clear hours all to herself, and her absence from the house won't be noticed, and when, without much difficulty, she can catch a train leaving Huxwell for Wreford. Well, she'll get to Wreford safe enough; but from Wreford she'll be followed every step of the way she goes. Only yesterday I set a man on there—a keen fellow at this sort of thing—and gave him full directions; and he'll hunt her down to her hole properly. Taken nothing with her, do you say? What does that matter? She thinks she'll find all she wants where she's going—'the feathered nest' I spoke to you about this morning. Ha! ha! Well, instead of stepping into it, as she fancies she will, she'll walk straight into a detective's arms, and land her pal there into the bargain. There'll be two of them netted before another forty-eight hours are over our heads, or my name's not Jeremiah Bates."

"What are you going to do now?" asked Loveday, as the man finished his long speech.

"Now! I'm back to the "King's Head" to wait for a telegram from my colleague at Wreford. Once he's got her in front of him he'll give me instructions at what point to meet him. You see, Huxwell being such an out-of-the-way place, and only one train leaving between 7.30 and 10.15, makes us really positive that Wreford must be the girl's destination and relieves my mind from all anxiety on the matter."

"Does it?" answered Loveday gravely. "I can see another possible destination for the girl—the stream that runs through the wood we drove past this morning. Good night, Mr. Bates, it's cold out here. Of course so soon as you have any news you'll send it up to Sir George."

The household sat up late that night, but no news was received of Stephanie from any quarter. Mr. Bates had impressed upon Sir George the ill-advisability of setting up a hue and cry after the girl that might possibly reach her ears and scare her from joining the person whom he was pleased to designate as her "pal."

"We want to follow her silently, Sir George, silently as, the shadow follows the man," he had said grandiloquently, "and then we shall come upon the two, and I trust upon their booty also." Sir George in his turn had impressed Mr. Bates's wishes upon his household, and if it had not been for Loveday's message, dispatched early in the evening to young Holt, not a soul outside the house would have known of Stephanie's disappearance.

Loveday was stirring early the next morning, and the eight o'clock train for Wreford numbered her among its passengers. Before starting, she dispatched a telegram to her chief in Lynch Court. It read rather oddly, as follows:—

Cracker fired. Am just starting for Wreford. Will wire to you from there.

L. B.

Oddly though it might read, Mr. Dyer did not need to refer to his cipher book to interpret it. "Cracker fired" was the easily remembered equivalent for "clue found" in the detective phraseology of the office.

"Well, she has been quick enough about it this time!" he soliquised as he speculated in his own mind over what the purport of the next telegram might be.

Half an hour later there came to him a constable from Scotland Yard to tell him of Stephanie's disappearance and the conjectures that were rife on the matter, and he then, not unnaturally, read Loveday's telegram by the light of this information, and concluded that the clue in her hands related to the discovery of Stephanie's whereabouts as well as to that of her guilt.

A telegram received a little later on, however, was to turn this theory upside down. It was, like the former one, worded in the enigmatic language current in the Lynch Court establishment, but as it was a lengthier and more intricate message, it sent Mr. Dyer at once to his cipher book.

"Wonderful! She has cut them all out this time!" was Mr. Dyer's exclamation as he read and interpreted the final word.

In another ten minutes he had given over his office to the charge of his head clerk for the day, and was rattling along the streets in a hansom in the direction of Bishopsgate Station.

There he was lucky enough to catch a train just starting for Wreford.

"The event of the day," he muttered, as he settled himself comfortably in a corner seat, "will be the return journey when she tells me, bit by bit, how she has worked it all out."

It was not until close upon three o'clock in the afternoon that he arrived at the old-fashioned market town of Wreford. It chanced to be cattle-market day, and the station was crowded with drovers and farmers. Outside the station Loveday was waiting for him, as she had told him in her telegram that she would, in a four-wheeler.

"It's all right," she said to him as he got in; "he can't get away, even if he had an idea that we were after him. Two of the local police are waiting outside the house door with a warrant for his arrest, signed by a magistrate. I did not, however, see why the Lynch Court office should not have the credit of the thing, and so telegraphed to you to conduct the arrest."

They drove through the High Street to the outskirts of the town, where the shops became intermixed with private houses let out in offices. The cab pulled up outside one of these, and two policemen in plain clothes came forward, and touched their hats to Mr. Dyer.

"He's in there now, sir, doing his office work," said one of the men pointing to a door, just within the entrance, on which was printed in black letters, "The United Kingdom Cab-drivers' Beneficent Association." "I hear however, that this is the last time he will be found there, as a week ago he gave notice to leave."

As the man finished speaking, a man, evidently of the cab-driving fraternity, came up the steps. He stared curiously at the little group just within the entrance, and then chinking his money in his hand, passed on to the office as if to pay his subscription.

"Will you be good enough to tell Mr. Emmett in there," said Mr. Dyer, addressing the man, "that a gentleman outside wishes to speak with him."

The man nodded and passed into the office. As the door opened, it disclosed to view an old gentleman seated at a desk apparently writing receipts for money. A little in his rear at his right hand, sat a young and decidedly good-looking man, at a table on which were placed various little piles of silver and pence. The get-up of this young man was gentleman-like, and his manner was affable and pleasant as he responded, with a nod and a smile, to the cab-driver's message.

"I sha'n't be a minute," he said to his colleague at the other desk, as he rose and crossed the room towards the door.

But once outside that door it was closed firmly behind him, and he found himself in the centre of three stalwart individuals, one of whom informed him that he held in his hand a warrant for the arrest of Harry Emmett on the charge of complicity in the Craigen Court robbery, and that he had "better come along quietly, for resistance would be useless."

Emmett seemed convinced of the latter fact. He grew deadly white for a moment, then recovered himself.

"Will someone have the kindness to fetch my hat and coat," he said in a lofty manner. "I don't see why I should be made to catch my death of cold because some other people have seen fit to make asses of themselves."

His hat and coat were fetched, and he was handed into the cab between the two officials.

"Let me give you a word of warning, young man," said Mr. Dyer, closing the cab door and looking in for a moment through the window at Emmett. "I don't suppose it's a punishable offence to leave a black bag on an old maid's doorstep, but let me tell you, if it had not been for that black bag you might have got clean off with your spoil."

Emmett, the irrepressible, had his answer ready. He lifted his hat ironically to Mr. Dyer; "You might have put it more neatly, guv'nor," he said; "if I had been in your place I would have said: 'Young man, you are being justly punished for your misdeeds; you have been taking off your fellow-creatures all your life long, and now they are taking off you.'"

Mr. Dyer's duty that day did not end with the depositing of Harry Emmett in the local jail. The search through Emmett's lodgings and effects had to be made, and at this he was naturally present. About a third of the lost jewellery was found there, and from this it was consequently concluded that his accomplices in the crime had considered that he had borne a third of the risk and of the danger of it.

Letters and various memoranda discovered in the rooms, eventually led to the detection of those accomplices, and although Lady Cathrow was doomed to lose the greater part of her valuable property, she had ultimately the satisfaction of knowing that each one of the thieves received a sentence proportionate to his crime.

It was not until close upon midnight that Mr. Dyer found himself seated in the train, facing Miss Brooke, and had leisure to ask for the links in the chain of reasoning that had led her in so remarkable a manner to connect the finding of a black bag, with insignificant contents, with an extensive robbery of valuable jewellery.

Loveday explained the whole thing, easily, naturally, step by step in her usual methodical manner.

"I read," she said, "as I dare say a great many other people did, the account of the two things in the same newspaper, on the same day, and I detected, as I dare say a great many other people did not, a sense of fun in the principal actor in each incident. I notice while all people are agreed as to the variety of motives that instigate crime, very few allow sufficient margin for variety of character in the criminal. We are apt to imagine that he stalks about the world with a bundle of deadly motives under his arm, and cannot picture him at his work with a twinkle in his eye and a keen sense of fun, such as honest folk have sometimes when at work at their calling."

Here Mr. Dyer gave a little grunt; it might have been either of assent or dissent.

Loveday went on:

"Of course, the ludicrousness of the diction of the letter found in the bag would be apparent to the most casual reader; to me the high falutin sentences sounded in addition strangely familiar; I had heard or read them somewhere I felt sure, although where I could not at first remember. They rang in my ears, and it was not altogether out of idle curiosity that I went to Scotland Yard to see the bag and its contents, and to copy, with a slip of tracing paper, a line or two of the letter. When I found that the handwriting of this letter was not identical with that of the translations found in the bag, I was confirmed in my impression that the owner of the bag was not the writer of the letter; that possibly the bag and its contents had been appropriated from some railway station for some distinct purpose; and, that purpose accomplished, the appropriator no longer wished to be burthened with it, and disposed of it in the readiest fashion that suggested itself. The letter, it seemed to me, had been begun with the intention of throwing the police off the scent, but the irrepressible spirit of fun that had induced the writer to deposit his clerical adjuncts upon an old maid's doorstep had proved too strong for him here, and had carried him away, and the letter that was intended to be pathetic ended in being comic."

"Very ingenious, so far," murmured Mr. Dyer: "I've no doubt when the contents of the bag are widely made known through advertisements a claimant will come forward, and your theory be found correct."

"When I returned from Scotland Yard," Loveday continued, "I found your note, asking me to go round and see you respecting the big jewel robbery. Before I did so I thought it best to read once more the newspaper account of the case, so that I might be well up in its details. When I came to the words that the thief had written across the door of the safe, 'To be Let, Unfurnished,' they at once connected themselves in my mind with the 'dying kiss to my Marchioness Mother,' and the solemn warning against the race-course and the book-maker, of the black-bag letter-writer. Then, all in a flash, the whole thing became clear to me. Some two or three years back my professional duties necessitated my frequent attendance at certain low class penny-readings, given in the South London slums. At these penny-readings young shop-assistants, and others of their class, glad of an opportunity for exhibiting their accomplishments, declaim with great vigour; and, as a rule, select pieces which their very mixed audience might be supposed to appreciate. During my attendance at these meetings, it seemed to me that one book of selected readings was a great favourite among the reciters, and I took the trouble to buy it. Here it is."

Here Loveday took from her cloak-pocket "The Reciter's Treasury," and handed it to her companion.

"Now," she said, "if you will run your eye down the index column you will find the titles of those pieces to which I wish to draw your attention. The first is 'The Suicide's Farewell;' the second, 'The Noble Convict;' the third, 'To be Let, Unfurnished.'"

"By Jove! so it is!" exclaimed Mr. Dyer.

"In the first of these pieces, 'The Suicide's Farewell,' occur the expressions with which the black-bag letter begins—'The fatal day has arrived,' etc., the warnings against gambling, and the allusions to the 'poor lifeless body.' In the second, 'The Noble Convict,' occur the allusions to the aristocratic relations and the dying kiss to the marchioness mother. The third piece, 'To be Let, Unfurnished,' is a foolish little poem enough, although I dare say it has often raised a laugh in a not too-discriminating audience. It tells how a bachelor, calling at a house to enquire after rooms to be let unfurnished, falls in love with the daughter of the house, and offers her his heart, which, he says, is to be let unfurnished. She declines his offer, and retorts that she thinks his head must be to let unfurnished, too. With these three pieces before me, it was not difficult to see a thread of connection between the writer of the black-bag letter and the thief who wrote across the empty safe at Craigen Court. Following this thread, I unearthed the story of Harry Emmett—footman, reciter, general lover and scamp. Subsequently I compared the writing on my tracing paper with that on the safe-door, and, allowing for the difference between a bit of chalk and a steel nib, came to the conclusion that there could be but little doubt but what both were written by the same hand. Before that, however, I had obtained another, and what I consider the most important, link in my chain of evidence—how Emmett brought his clerical dress into use."

"Ah, how did you find out that now?" asked Mr. Dyer, leaning forward with his elbows on his knees.

"In the course of conversation with Mrs. Williams, whom I found to be a most communicative person, I elicited the names of the guests who had sat down to dinner on Christmas Eve. They were all people of undoubted respectability in the neighbourhood. Just before dinner was announced, she said, a young clergyman had presented himself at the front door, asking to speak with the Rector of the parish. The Rector, it seems, always dines at Craigen Court on Christmas Eve. The young clergyman's story was that he had been told by a certain clergyman, whose name he mentioned, that a curate was wanted in the parish, and he had traveled down from London to offer his services. He had been, he said, to the Rectory and had been told by the servants where the Rector was dining, and fearing to lose his chance of the curacy, had followed him to the Court. Now the Rector had been wanting a curate and had filled the vacancy only the previous week; he was a little inclined to be irate at this interruption to the evening's festivities, and told the young man that he didn't want a curate. When, however, he saw how disappointed the poor young fellow looked—I believe he shed a tear or two—his heart softened; he told him to sit down and rest in the hall before he attempted the walk back to the station, and said he would ask Sir George to send him out a glass of wine. the young man sat down in a chair immediately outside the room by which the thieves entered. Now I need not tell you who that young man was, nor suggest to your mind, I am sure, the idea that while the servant went to fetch him his wine, or, indeed, so soon as he saw the coast clear, he slipped into that little room and pulled back the catch of the window that admitted his confederates, who, no doubt, at that very moment were in hiding in the grounds. The housekeeper did not know whether this meek young curate had a black bag with him. Personally I have no doubt of the fact, nor that it contained the cap, cuffs, collar, and outer garments of Harry Emmett, which were most likely redonned before he returned to his lodgings at Wreford, where I should say he repacked the bag with its clerical contents, and wrote his serio-comic letter. This bag, I suppose, he must have deposited in the very early morning, before anyone was stirring, on the door-step of the house in the Easterbrook Road."

Mr. Dyer drew a long breath. In his heart was unmitigated admiration for his colleague's skill, which seemed to him to fall little short of inspiration. By-and-by, no doubt, he would sing her praises to the first person who came along with a hearty good will; he had not, however, the slightest intention of so singing them in her own ears—excessive praise was apt to have a bad effect on the rising practitioner.

So he contented himself with saying:

"Yes, very satisfactory. Now tell me how you hunted the fellow down to his diggings?"

"Oh, that was mere ABC work," answered Loveday. "Mrs. Williams told me he had left his place at Colonel James's about six months previously, and had told her he was going to look after his dear old grandmother, who kept a sweet stuff-shop; but where she could not remember. Having heard that Emmett's father was a cab-driver, my thoughts at once flew to the cabman's vernacular—you know something of it, no doubt—in which their provident association is designated by the phase, 'the dear old grandmother,' and the office where they make and receive their payments is styled 'the sweet stuff-shop.'"

"Ha, ha, ha! And good Mrs. Williams took it all literally, no doubt?"

"She did; and thought what a dear, kind-hearted fellow the young man was. Naturally I supposed there would be a branch of the association in the nearest market town, and a local trades' directory confirmed my supposition that there was one at Wreford. Bearing in mind where the black bag was found, it was not difficult to believe that young Emmett, possibly through his father's influence and his own prepossessing manners and appearance, had attained to some position of trust in the Wreford branch. I must confess I scarcely expected to find him as I did, on reaching the place, installed as receiver of the weekly moneys. Of course, I immediately put myself in communication with the police there, and the rest I think you know."

Mr. Dyer's enthusiasm refused to be longer restrained.

"It's capital, from first to last," he cried; "you've surpassed yourself this time!"

"The only thing that saddens me," said Loveday, "is the thought of the possible fate of that poor little Stephanie."

Loveday's anxieties on Stephanie's behalf were, however, to be put to flight before another twenty-four hours had passed. The first post on the following morning brought a letter from Mrs. Williams telling how the girl had been found before the night was over, half dead with cold and fright, on the verge of the stream running through Craigen Wood—"found too"—wrote the housekeeper, "by the very person who ought to have found her, young Holt, who was, and is so desperately in love with her. Thank goodness! at the last moment her courage failed her, and instead of throwing herself into the stream, she sank down, half-fainting, beside it. Holt took her straight home to his mother, and there, at the farm, she is now, being taken care of and petted generally by everyone."

THE MURDER AT TROYTE'S HILL

"Griffiths, of the Newcastle Constabulary, has the case in hand," said Mr. Dyer; "those Newcastle men are keen-witted, shrewd fellows, and very jealous of outside interference. They only sent to me under protest, as it were, because they wanted your sharp wits at work inside the house."

"I suppose throughout I am to work with Griffiths, not with you?" said Miss Brooke.

"Yes; when I have given you in outline the facts of the case, I simply have nothing more to do with it, and you must depend on Griffiths for any assistance of any sort that you may require."

Here, with a swing, Mr. Dyer opened his big ledger and turned rapidly over its leaves till he came to the heading "Troyte's Hill" and the date "September 6th."

"I'm all attention," said Loveday, leaning back in her chair in the attitude of a listener.

"The murdered man," resumed Mr. Dyer, "is a certain Alexander Henderson—usually known as old Sandy—lodge-keeper to Mr. Craven, of Troyte's Hill, Cumberland. The lodge consists merely of two rooms on the ground floor, a bedroom and a sitting-room; these Sandy occupied alone, having neither kith nor kin of any degree. On the morning of September 6th, some children going up to the house with milk from the farm, noticed that Sandy's bed-room window stood wide open. Curiosity prompted them to peep in; and then, to their horror, they saw old Sandy, in his night-shirt, lying dead on the floor, as if he had fallen backwards from the window. They raised an alarm; and on examination, it was found that death had ensued from a heavy blow on the temple, given either by a strong fist or some blunt instrument. The room, on being entered, presented a curious appearance. It was as if a herd of monkeys had been turned into it and allowed to work their impish will. Not an article of furniture remained in its place: the bed-clothes had been rolled into a bundle and stuffed into the chimney; the bedstead—a small iron one—lay on its side; the one chair in the room stood on the top of the table; fender and fire-irons lay across the washstand, whose basin was to be found in a farther corner, holding bolster and pillow. The clock stood on its head in the middle of the mantelpiece; and the small vases and ornaments, which flanked it on

CATHERINE LOUISA PIRKIS

either side, were walking, as it were, in a straight line towards the door. The old man's clothes had been rolled into a ball and thrown on the top of a high cupboard in which he kept his savings and whatever valuables he had. This cupboard, however, had not been meddled with, and its contents remained intact, so it was evident that robbery was not the motive for the crime. At the inquest, subsequently held, a verdict of 'willful murder' against some person or persons unknown was returned. The local police are diligently investigating the affair, but, as yet, no arrests have been made. The opinion that at present prevails in the neighbourhood is that the crime has been perpetrated by some lunatic, escaped or otherwise and enquiries are being made at the local asylums as to missing or lately released inmates. Griffiths, however, tells me that his suspicions set in another direction."

"Did anything of importance transpire at the inquest?"

"Nothing specially important. Mr. Craven broke down in giving his evidence when he alluded to the confidential relations that had always subsisted between Sandy and himself, and spoke of the last time that he had seen him alive. The evidence of the butler, and one or two of the female servants, seems clear enough, and they let fall something of a hint that Sandy was not altogether a favourite among them, on account of the overbearing manner in which he used his influence with his master. Young Mr. Craven, a youth of about nineteen, home from Oxford for the long vacation, was not present at the inquest; a doctor's certificate was put in stating that he was suffering from typhoid fever, and could not leave his bed without risk to his life. Now this young man is a thoroughly bad sort, and as much a gentleman-blackleg as it is possible for such a young fellow to be. It seems to Griffiths that there is something suspicious about this illness of his. He came back from Oxford on the verge of delirium tremens, pulled round from that, and then suddenly, on the day after the murder, Mrs. Craven rings the bell, announces that he has developed typhoid fever and orders a doctor to be sent for."

"What sort of man is Mr. Craven senior?"

"He seems to be a quiet old fellow, a scholar and learned philologist. Neither his neighbours nor his family see much of him; he almost lives in his study, writing a treatise, in seven or eight volumes, on comparative philology. He is not a rich man. Troyte's Hill, though it carries position in the county, is not a paying property, and Mr. Craven is unable to keep it up properly. I am told he has had to cut down expenses in all directions in order to send his son to college, and his daughter from first to last has been entirely educated by her mother. Mr. Craven was originally intended for the church, but for some reason or other, when his college career came to an end, he did not present himself for ordination—went out to Natal instead, where he obtained some civil appointment and where he remained for about fifteen years. Henderson was his servant during the latter portion of his Oxford career, and must have been greatly respected by him, for although the remuneration derived from his appointment at Natal was small, he paid Sandy a regular yearly allowance out of it. When, about ten years ago, he succeeded to Troyte's Hill, on the death of his elder brother, and returned home with his family, Sandy was immediately installed as lodge-keeper, and at so high a rate of pay that the butler's wages were cut down to meet it."

"Ah, that wouldn't improve the butler's feelings towards him," exclaimed Loveday.

Mr. Dyer went on: "But, in spite of his high wages, he doesn't appear to have troubled much about his duties as lodge-keeper, for they were performed, as a rule, by the gardener's boy, while he took his meals and passed his time at the house, and, speaking generally, put his finger into every pie. You know the old adage respecting the servant of twenty-one years' standing: 'Seven years my servant, seven years my equal, seven years my master.' Well, it appears to have held good in the case of Mr. Craven and Sandy. The old gentleman, absorbed in his philological studies, evidently let the reins slip through his fingers, and Sandy seems to have taken easy possession of them. The servants frequently had to go to him for orders, and he carried things, as a rule, with a high hand."

"Did Mrs. Craven never have a word to say on the matter?"

"I've not heard much about her. She seems to be a quiet sort of person. She is a Scotch missionary's daughter; perhaps she spends her time working for the Cape mission and that sort of thing."

"And young Mr. Craven: did he knock under to Sandy's rule?"

"Ah, now you're hitting the bull's eye and we come to Griffiths' theory. The young man and Sandy appear to have been at loggerheads ever since the Cravens took possession of Troyte's Hill. As a schoolboy Master Harry defied Sandy and threatened him with his hunting-crop; and subsequently, as a young man, has used strenuous endeavours to put the old servant in his place. On the day before the murder, Griffiths says, there was a terrible scene between the two, in which the young gentleman, in the presence of several witnesses, made use of strong language and threatened the old man's life. Now, Miss Brooke, I have told you all the circumstances of the case so far as I know them. For fuller particulars I must refer you to Griffiths. He, no doubt, will meet you at Grenfell—the nearest station to Troyte's Hill, and tell you in what capacity he has procured for you an entrance into the house. By-the-way, he has wired to me this morning that he hopes you will be able to save the Scotch express to-night."

Loveday expressed her readiness to comply with Mr. Griffiths' wishes.

"I shall be glad," said Mr. Dyer, as he shook hands with her at the office door, "to see you immediately on your return—that, however, I suppose, will not be yet awhile. This promises, I fancy, to be a longish affair?" This was said interrogatively.

"I haven't the least idea on the matter," answered Loveday. "I start on my work without theory of any sort—in fact, I may say, with my mind a perfect blank."

And anyone who had caught a glimpse of her blank, expressionless features, as she said this, would have taken her at her word.

Grenfell, the nearest post-town to Troyte's Hill, is a fairly busy, populous little town—looking south towards the black country, and northwards to low, barren hills. Pre-eminent among these stands Troyte's Hill, famed in the old days as a border keep, and possibly at a still earlier date as a Druid stronghold.

At a small inn at Grenfell, dignified by the title of "The Station Hotel," Mr. Griffiths, of the Newcastle constabulary, met Loveday and still further initiated her into the mysteries of the Troyte's Hill murder.

"A little of the first excitement has subsided," he said, after preliminary greetings had been exchanged; "but still the wildest rumours are flying about and repeated as solemnly as if they were Gospel truths. My chief here and my colleagues generally adhere to their first conviction, that the criminal is some suddenly crazed tramp or else an escaped lunatic, and they are confident that sooner or later we shall come upon his traces. Their theory is that Sandy, hearing some strange noise at the Park Gates, put his head out of the window to ascertain the cause and immediately had his death blow dealt him; then they suppose that the lunatic scrambled into the room through the window and exhausted his frenzy by turning things generally upside down. They refuse altogether to share my suspicions respecting young Mr. Craven."

Mr. Griffiths was a tall, thin-featured man, with iron-grey hair, but so close to his head that it refused to do anything but stand on end. This gave a somewhat comic expression to the upper portion of his face and clashed oddly with the melancholy look that his mouth habitually wore.

"I have made all smooth for you at Troyte's Hill," he presently went on. "Mr. Craven is not wealthy enough to allow himself the luxury of a family lawyer, so he occasionally employs the services of Messrs. Wells and Sugden, lawyers in this place, and who, as it happens, have, off and on, done a good deal of business for me. It was through them I heard that Mr. Craven was anxious to secure the assistance of an amanuensis. I immediately offered your services, stating that you were a friend of mine, a lady of impoverished means, who would gladly undertake the duties for the munificent sum of a guinea a month, with board and lodging. The old gentleman at once jumped at the offer, and is anxious for you to be at Troyte's Hill at once."

Loveday expressed her satisfaction with the programme that Mr. Griffiths had sketched for her, then she had a few questions to ask.

"Tell me," she said, "what led you, in the first instance, to suspect young Mr. Craven of the crime?"

"The footing on which he and Sandy stood towards each other, and the terrible scene that occurred between them only the day before the murder," answered Griffiths, promptly. "Nothing of this, however, was elicited at the inquest, where a very fair face was put on Sandy's relations with the whole of the Craven family. I have subsequently unearthed a good deal respecting the private life of Mr. Harry Craven, and, among other things, I have found out that on the night of the murder he left the house shortly after ten o'clock, and no one, so far as I have been able to ascertain, knows at what hour he returned. Now I must draw your attention, Miss Brooke, to the fact that at the inquest the medical evidence went to prove that the murder had been committed between ten and eleven at night."

"Do you surmise, then, that the murder was a planned thing on the part of this young man?"

"I do. I believe that he wandered about the grounds until Sandy shut himself in for the night, then aroused him by some outside noise, and, when the old man looked out to ascertain the cause, dealt him a blow with a bludgeon or loaded stick, that caused his death."

"A cold-blooded crime that, for a boy of nineteen?"

"Yes. He's a good-looking, gentlemanly youngster, too, with manners as mild as milk, but from all accounts is as full of wickedness as an egg is full of meat. Now, to come to another point—if, in connection with these ugly facts, you take into consideration the suddenness of his illness, I think you'll admit that it bears a suspicious appearance and might reasonably give rise to the surmise that it was a plant on his part, in order to get out of the inquest."

"Who is the doctor attending him?"

"A man called Waters; not much of a practitioner, from all accounts, and no doubt he feels himself highly honoured in being summoned to Troyte's Hill. The Cravens, it seems, have no family doctor. Mrs. Craven, with her missionary experience, is half a doctor herself, and never calls in one except in a serious emergency."

"The certificate was in order, I suppose?"

"Undoubtedly. And, as if to give colour to the gravity of the case, Mrs. Craven sent a message down to the servants, that if any of them were afraid of the infection they could at once go to their homes. Several of the maids, I believe, took advantage of her permission, and packed their boxes. Miss Craven, who is a delicate girl, was sent away with her maid to stay with friends at Newcastle, and Mrs. Craven isolated herself with her patient in one of the disused wings of the house."

"Has anyone ascertained whether Miss Craven arrived at her destination at Newcastle?"

Griffiths drew his brows together in thought.

"I did not see any necessity for such a thing," he answered. "I don't quite follow you. What do you mean to imply?"

"Oh, nothing. I don't suppose it matters much: it might have been interesting as a side-issue." She broke off for a moment, then added:

"Now tell me a little about the butler, the man whose wages were cut down to increase Sandy's pay."

"Old John Hales? He's a thoroughly worthy, respectable man; he was butler for five or six years to Mr. Craven's brother, when he was master of Troyte's Hill, and then took duty under this Mr. Craven. There's no ground for suspicion in that quarter. Hales's exclamation when he heard of the murder is quite enough to stamp him as an innocent man: 'Serve the old idiot right,' he cried: 'I couldn't pump up a tear for him if I tried for a month of Sundays!' Now I take it, Miss Brooke, a guilty man wouldn't dare make such a speech as that!"

"You think not?"

Griffiths stared at her. "I'm a little disappointed in her," he thought. "I'm afraid her powers have been slightly exaggerated if she can't see such a straight-forward thing as that."

Aloud he said, a little sharply, "Well, I don't stand alone in my thinking. No one yet has breathed a word against Hales, and if they did, I've no doubt he could prove an *alibi* without any trouble, for he lives in the house, and everyone has a good word for him."

"I suppose Sandy's lodge has been put into order by this time?"

"Yes; after the inquest, and when all possible evidence had been taken, everything was put straight."

"At the inquest it was stated that no marks of footsteps could be traced in any direction?"

"The long drought we've had would render such a thing impossible, let alone the fact that Sandy's lodge stands right on the graveled drive, without flower-beds or grass borders of any sort around it. But look here, Miss Brooke, don't you be wasting your time over the lodge and its surroundings. Every iota of fact on that matter has been gone through over and over again by me and my chief. What we want you to do is to go straight into the house and concentrate attention on Master Harry's sick-room, and find out what's going on there. What he did outside the house on the night of the 6th, I've no doubt I shall be able to find out for myself. Now, Miss Brooke, you've asked me no end of questions, to which I have replied as fully as it was in my power to do; will you be good enough to answer one question that I wish to put, as straightforwardly as I have answered yours? You have had fullest particulars given you of the condition of Sandy's room when the police entered it on the morning after the murder. No doubt, at the present moment, you can see it all in your mind's eye—the bedstead on its side, the clock on its head, the bed-clothes half-way up the chimney, the little vases and ornaments walking in a straight line towards the door?"

Loveday bowed her head.

"Very well, Now will you be good enough to tell me what this scene of confusion recalls to your mind before anything else?"

"The room of an unpopular Oxford freshman after a raid upon it by undergrads," answered Loveday promptly.

Mr. Griffiths rubbed his hands.

"Quite so!" he exclaimed. "I see, after all, we are one at heart in this matter, in spite of a little surface disagreement of ideas. Depend upon it, by-and-bye, like the engineers tunneling from different quarters under

CATHERINE LOUISA PIRKIS

the Alps, we shall meet at the same point and shake hands. By-the-way, I have arranged for daily communication between us through the postboy who takes the letters to Troyte's Hill. He is trustworthy, and any letter you give him for me will find its way into my hands within the hour."

It was about three o'clock in the afternoon when Loveday drove in through the park gates of Troyte's Hill, past the lodge where old Sandy had met with his death. It was a pretty little cottage, covered with Virginia creeper and wild honeysuckle, and showing no outward sign of the tragedy that had been enacted within.

The park and pleasure-grounds of Troyte's Hill were extensive, and the house itself was a somewhat imposing red brick structure, built, possibly, at the time when Dutch William's taste had grown popular in the country. Its frontage presented a somewhat forlorn appearance, its centre windows—a square of eight—alone seeming to show signs of occupation. With the exception of two windows at the extreme end of the bedroom floor of the north wing, where, possibly, the invalid and his mother were located, and two windows at the extreme end of the ground floor of the south wing, which Loveday ascertained subsequently were those of Mr. Craven's study, not a single window in either wing owned blind or curtain. The wings were extensive, and it was easy to understand that at the extreme end of the one the fever patient would be isolated from the rest of the household, and that at the extreme end of the other Mr. Craven could secure the quiet and freedom from interruption which, no doubt, were essential to the due prosecution of his philological studies.

Alike on the house and ill-kept grounds were present the stamp of the smallness of the income of the master and owner of the place. The terrace, which ran the length of the house in front, and on to which every window on the ground floor opened, was miserably out of repair: not a lintel or door-post, window-ledge or balcony but what seemed to cry aloud for the touch of the painter. "Pity me! I have seen better days," Loveday could fancy written as a legend across the red-brick porch that gave entrance to the old house.

The butler, John Hales, admitted Loveday, shouldered her portmanteau and told her he would show her to her room. He was a tall, powerfully-built man, with a ruddy face and dogged expression of countenance. It was easy to understand that, off and on, there must have been many a sharp encounter between him and old Sandy. He treated Loveday in an easy, familiar fashion, evidently considering that an amanuensis took much the same rank as a nursery governess—that is to say, a little below a lady's maid and a little above a house-maid.

"We're short of hands, just now," he said, in broad Cumberland dialect, as he led the way up the wide stair case. "Some of the lasses downstairs took fright at the fever and went home. Cook and I are single-handed, for Moggie, the only maid left, has been told off to wait on Madam and Master Harry. I hope you're not afeared of fever?"

Loveday explained that she was not, and asked if the room at the extreme end of the north wing was the one assigned to "Madam and Master Harry."

"Yes," said the man; "it's convenient for sick nursing; there's a flight of stairs runs straight down from it to the kitchen quarters. We put all Madam wants at the foot of those stairs and Moggie herself never enters the sick-room. I take it you'll not be seeing Madam for many a day, yet awhile."

"When shall I see Mr. Craven? At dinner to-night?"

"That's what naebody could say," answered Hales. "He may not come out of his study till past midnight; sometimes he sits there till two or three in the morning. Shouldn't advise you to wait till he wants his dinner—better have a cup of tea and a chop sent up to you. Madam never waits for him at any meal."

As he finished speaking he deposited the portmanteau outside one of the many doors opening into the gallery.

"This is Miss Craven's room," he went on; "cook and me thought you'd better have it, as it would want less getting ready than the other rooms, and work is work when there are so few hands to do it. Oh, my stars! I do declare there is cook putting it straight for you now." The last sentence was added as the opened door laid bare to view, the cook, with a duster in her hand, polishing a mirror; the bed had been made, it is true, but otherwise the room must have been much as Miss Craven left it, after a hurried packing up.

To the surprise of the two servants Loveday took the matter very lightly.

"I have a special talent for arranging rooms and would prefer getting this one straight for myself," she said. "Now, if you will go and get ready that chop and cup of tea we were talking about just now, I shall think it much kinder than if you stayed here doing what I can so easily do for myself."

When, however, the cook and butler had departed in company, Loveday showed no disposition to exercise the "special talent" of which she had boasted.

She first carefully turned the key in the lock and then proceeded to make a thorough and minute investigation of every corner of the room. Not an article of furniture, not an ornament or toilet accessory, but what was lifted from its place and carefully scrutinized. Even the ashes in the grate, the debris of the last fire made there, were raked over and well looked through.

This careful investigation of Miss Craven's late surroundings occupied in all about three quarters of an hour, and Loveday, with her hat in her hand, descended the stairs to see Hales crossing the hall to the dining-room with the promised cup of tea and chop.

In silence and solitude she partook of the simple repast in a dining-hall that could with ease have banqueted a hundred and fifty guests.

"Now for the grounds before it gets dark," she said to herself, as she noted that already the outside shadows were beginning to slant.

The dining-hall was at the back of the house; and here, as in the front, the windows, reaching to the ground, presented easy means of egress. The flower-garden was on this side of the house and sloped downhill to a pretty stretch of well-wooded country.

Loveday did not linger here even to admire, but passed at once round the south corner of the house to the windows which she had ascertained, by a careless question to the butler, were those of Mr. Craven's study.

Very cautiously she drew near them, for the blinds were up, the curtains drawn back. A side glance, however, relieved her apprehensions, for it showed her the occupant of the room, seated in an easy-chair, with his back to the windows. From the length of his outstretched limbs he was evidently a tall man. His hair was silvery and curly, the lower part of his face was hidden from her view by the chair, but she could see one hand was pressed tightly across his eyes and brows. The whole attitude was that of a man absorbed in deep thought. The room was comfortably furnished, but presented an appearance of disorder from the books and manuscripts scattered in all directions. A whole pile of torn fragments of foolscap sheets, overflowing from a waste-paper basket beside the writing-table, seemed to proclaim the fact that the scholar had of late grown weary of, or else dissatisfied with his work, and had condemned it freely.

Although Loveday stood looking in at this window for over five minutes, not the faintest sign of life did that tall, reclining figure give, and it would have been as easy to believe him locked in sleep as in thought.

From here she turned her steps in the direction of Sandy's lodge. As Griffiths had said, it was graveled up to its doorstep. The blinds were closely drawn, and it presented the ordinary appearance of a disused cottage.

A narrow path beneath over-arching boughs of cherry-laurel and arbutus, immediately facing the lodge, caught her eye, and down this she at once turned her footsteps.

This path led, with many a wind and turn, through a belt of shrubbery that skirted the frontage of Mr. Craven's grounds, and eventually, after much zig-zagging, ended in close proximity to the stables. As Loveday entered it, she seemed literally to leave daylight behind her.

"I feel as if I were following the course of a circuitous mind," she said to herself as the shadows closed around her. "I could not fancy Sir Isaac Newton or Bacon planning or delighting in such a wind-about-alley as this!"

The path showed greyly in front of her out of the dimness. On and on she followed it; here and there the roots of the old laurels, struggling out of the ground, threatened to trip her up. Her eyes, however, had now grown accustomed to the half-gloom, and not a detail of her surroundings escaped her as she went along.

A bird flew from out the thicket on her right hand with a startled cry. A dainty little frog leaped out of her way into the shriveled leaves lying below the laurels. Following the movements of this frog, her eye was caught by something black and solid among those leaves. What was it? A bundle—a shiny black coat? Loveday knelt down, and using her hands to assist her eyes, found that they came into contact with the dead, stiffened body of a beautiful black retriever. She parted, as well as she was able, the lower boughs of the evergreens, and minutely examined the poor animal. Its eyes were still open, though glazed and bleared, and its death had, undoubtedly, been caused by the blow of some blunt, heavy instrument, for on one side its skull was almost battered in.

"Exactly the death that was dealt to Sandy," she thought, as she groped hither and thither beneath the trees in hopes of lighting upon the weapon of destruction.

She searched until increasing darkness warned her that search was useless. Then, still following the zig-zagging path, she made her way out by the stables and thence back to the house.

She went to bed that night without having spoken to a soul beyond the cook and butler. The next morning, however, Mr. Craven introduced himself to her across the breakfast-table. He was a man of really handsome personal appearance, with a fine carriage of the head and shoulders, and eyes that had a forlorn, appealing look in them. He entered the room with an air of great energy, apologized to Loveday for the absence of his wife, and for his own remissness in not being in the way to receive her on the previous day. Then he bade her make herself at home at the breakfast-table, and expressed his delight in having found a coadjutor in his work.

"I hope you understand what a great—a stupendous work it is?" he added, as he sank into a chair. "It is a work that will leave its impress upon thought in all the ages to come. Only a man who has studied comparative philology as I have for the past thirty years, could gauge the magnitude of the task I have set myself."

With the last remark, his energy seemed spent, and he sank back in his chair, covering his eyes with his hand in precisely the same attitude as that in which Loveday had seen him over-night, and utterly oblivious of the fact that breakfast was before him and a stranger-guest seated at table. The butler entered with another dish. "Better go on with your breakfast," he whispered to Loveday, "he may sit like that for another hour."

He placed his dish in front of his master.

"Captain hasn't come back yet, sir," he said, making an effort to arouse him from his reverie.

"Eh, what?" said Mr. Craven, for a moment lifting his hand from his eyes.

"Captain, sir—the black retriever," repeated the man.

The pathetic look in Mr. Craven's eyes deepened.

"Ah, poor Captain!" he murmured; "the best dog I ever had."

Then he again sank back in his chair, putting his hand to his forehead.

The butler made one more effort to arouse him.

"Madam sent you down a newspaper, sir, that she thought you would like to see," he shouted almost into his master's ear, and at the same time laid the morning's paper on the table beside his plate.

"Confound you! leave it there," said Mr. Craven irritably. "Fools! dolts that you all are! With your trivialities and interruptions you are sending me out of the world with my work undone!"

And again he sank back in his chair, closed his eyes and became lost to his surroundings.

Loveday went on with her breakfast. She changed her place at table to one on Mr. Craven's right hand, so that the newspaper sent down for his perusal lay between his plate and hers. It was folded into an oblong shape, as if it were wished to direct attention to a certain portion of a certain column.

A clock in a corner of the room struck the hour with a loud, resonant stroke. Mr. Craven gave a start and rubbed his eyes.

"Eh, what's this?" he said. "What meal are we at?" He looked around with a bewildered air. "Eh!—who are you?" he went on, staring hard at Loveday. "What are you doing here? Where's Nina?—Where's Harry?"

Loveday began to explain, and gradually recollection seemed to come back to him.

"Ah, yes, yes," he said. "I remember; you've come to assist me with my great work. You promised, you know, to help me out of the hole I've got into. Very enthusiastic, I remember they said you were, on certain abstruse points in comparative philology. Now, Miss—Miss—I've forgotten your name—tell me a little of what you know about the elemental sounds of speech that are common to all languages. Now, to how many would you reduce those elemental sounds—to six, eight, nine? No, we won't discuss the matter here, the cups and saucers distract me. Come into my den at the other end of the house; we'll have perfect quiet there."

And utterly ignoring the fact that he had not as yet broken his fast, he rose from the table, seized Loveday by the wrist, and led her out of the room and down the long corridor that led through the south wing to his study.

But seated in that study his energy once more speedily exhausted itself.

He placed Loveday in a comfortable chair at his writing-table, consulted her taste as to pens, and spread a sheet of foolscap before her. Then he settled himself in his easy-chair, with his back to the light, as if he were about to dictate folios to her.

In a loud, distinct voice he repeated the title of his learned work, then its sub-division, then the number and heading of the chapter that was at present engaging his attention. Then he put his hand to his head. "It's the elemental sounds that are my stumbling-block," he said. "Now, how on earth is it possible to get a notion of a sound of agony that is not in part a sound of terror? or a sound of surprise that is not in part a sound of either joy or sorrow?"

With this his energies were spent, and although Loveday remained seated in that study from early morning till daylight began to fade, she had not ten sentences to show for her day's work as amanuensis.

Loveday in all spent only two clear days at Troyte's Hill.

On the evening of the first of those days Detective Griffiths received, through the trustworthy post-boy, the following brief note from her:

> I have found out that Hales owed Sandy close upon
> a hundred pounds, which he had borrowed at various
> times. I don't know whether you will think this fact of any
> importance.
>
> L. B.

Mr. Griffiths repeated the last sentence blankly. "If Harry Craven were put upon his defence, his counsel, I take it, would consider the fact of first importance," he muttered. And for the remainder of that day Mr. Griffiths went about his work in a perturbed state of mind, doubtful whether to hold or to let go his theory concerning Harry Craven's guilt.

The next morning there came another brief note from Loveday which ran thus:

> "As a matter of collateral interest, find out if a person, calling
> himself Harold Cousins, sailed two days ago from London
> Docks for Natal in the *Bonnie Dundee?*"

To this missive Loveday received, in reply, the following somewhat lengthy dispatch:

> I do not quite see the drift of your last note, but have wired
> to our agents in London to carry out its suggestion. On my
> part, I have important news to communicate. I have found
> out what Harry Craven's business out of doors was on the
> night of the murder, and at my instance a warrant has been
> issued for his arrest. This warrant it will be my duty to serve
> on him in the course of to-day. Things are beginning to look
> very black against him, and I am convinced his illness is all
> a sham. I have seen Waters, the man who is supposed to be
> attending him, and have driven him into a corner and made
> him admit that he has only seen young Craven once—on
> the first day of his illness—and that he gave his certificate

entirely on the strength of what Mrs. Craven told him of her son's condition. On the occasion of this, his first and only visit, the lady, it seems, also told him that it would not be necessary for him to continue his attendance, as she quite felt herself competent to treat the case, having had so much experience in fever cases among the blacks at Natal.

As I left Waters's house, after eliciting this important information, I was accosted by a man who keeps a low-class inn in the place, McQueen by name. He said that he wished to speak to me on a matter of importance. To make a long story short, this McQueen stated that on the night of the sixth, shortly after eleven o'clock, Harry Craven came to his house, bringing with him a valuable piece of plate—a handsome epergne—and requested him to lend him a hundred pounds on it, as he hadn't a penny in his pocket. McQueen complied with his request to the extent of ten sovereigns, and now, in a fit of nervous terror, comes to me to confess himself a receiver of stolen goods and play the honest man! He says he noticed that the young gentleman was very much agitated as he made the request, and he also begged him to mention his visit to no one. Now, I am curious to learn how Master Harry will get over the fact that he passed the lodge at the hour at which the murder was most probably committed; or how he will get out of the dilemma of having repassed the lodge on his way back to the house, and not noticed the wide-open window with the full moon shining down on it?

Another word! Keep out of the way when I arrive at the house, somewhere between two and three in the afternoon, to serve the warrant. I do not wish your professional capacity to get wind, for you will most likely yet be of some use to us in the house.

S.G.

Loveday read this note, seated at Mr. Craven's writing-table, with the old gentleman himself reclining motionless beside her in his easy-chair. A little smile played about the corners of her mouth as she read over again the words—"for you will most likely yet be of some use to us in the house."

Loveday's second day in Mr. Craven's study promised to be as unfruitful as the first. For fully an hour after she had received Griffiths' note, she sat at the writing-table with her pen in her hand, ready to transcribe Mr. Craven's inspirations. Beyond, however, the phrase, muttered with closed eyes—"It's all here, in my brain, but I can't put it into words"—not a half-syllable escaped his lips.

At the end of that hour the sound of footsteps on the outside gravel made her turn her head towards the window. It was Griffiths approaching with two constables. She heard the hall door opened to admit them, but, beyond that, not a sound reached her ear, and she realized how fully she was cut off from communication with the rest of the household at the farther end of this unoccupied wing.

Mr. Craven, still reclining in his semi-trance, evidently had not the faintest suspicion that so important an event as the arrest of his only son on a charge of murder was about to be enacted in the house.

Meantime, Griffiths and his constables had mounted the stairs leading to the north wing, and were being guided through the corridors to the sick-room by the flying figure of Moggie, the maid.

"Hoot, mistress!" cried the girl, "here are three men coming up the stairs—policemen, every one of them—will ye come and ask them what they be wanting?"

Outside the door of the sick-room stood Mrs. Craven—a tall, sharp-featured woman with sandy hair going rapidly grey.

"What is the meaning of this? What is your business here?" she said haughtily, addressing Griffiths, who headed the party.

Griffiths respectfully explained what his business was, and requested her to stand on one side that he might enter her son's room.

"This is my daughter's room; satisfy yourself of the fact," said the lady, throwing back the door as she spoke.

And Griffiths and his confrères entered, to find pretty Miss Craven, looking very white and scared, seated beside a fire in a long flowing robe de chambre.

Griffiths departed in haste and confusion, without the chance of a professional talk with Loveday. That afternoon saw him telegraphing wildly in all directions, and dispatching messengers in all quarters. Finally he spent over an hour drawing up an elaborate report to his chief at Newcastle, assuring him of the identity of one, Harold Cousins, who had sailed in the *Bonnie Dundee* for Natal, with Harry Craven, of Troyte's Hill, and advising that the police authorities in that far-away district should be immediately communicated with.

The ink had not dried on the pen with which this report was written before a note, in Loveday's writing, was put into his hand.

Loveday evidently had had some difficulty in finding a messenger for this note, for it was brought by a gardener's boy, who informed Griffiths that the lady had said he would receive a gold sovereign if he delivered the letter all right.

Griffiths paid the boy and dismissed him, and then proceeded to read Loveday's communication.

It was written hurriedly in pencil, and ran as follows:

"Things are getting critical here. Directly you receive this, come up to the house with two of your men, and post yourselves anywhere in the grounds where you can see and not be seen. There will be no difficulty in this, for it will be dark by the time you are able to get there. I am not sure whether I shall want your aid to-night, but you had better keep in the grounds until morning, in case of need; and above all, never once lose sight of the study windows." (This was underscored.) "If I put a lamp with a green shade in one of those windows, do not lose a moment in entering by that window, which I will contrive to keep unlocked."

Detective Griffiths rubbed his forehead—rubbed his eyes, as he finished reading this.

"Well, I daresay it's all right," he said, "but I'm bothered, that's all, and for the life of me I can't see one step of the way she is going."

He looked at his watch: the hands pointed to a quarter past six. The short September day was drawing rapidly to a close. A good five miles lay between him and Troyte's Hill—there was evidently not a moment to lose.

At the very moment that Griffiths, with his two constables, were once more starting along the Grenfell High Road behind the best horse they could procure, Mr. Craven was rousing himself from his long slumber, and beginning to look around him. That slumber, however, though long, had not been a peaceful one, and it was sundry of the old gentleman's muttered exclamations, as he had started uneasily in his sleep, that had caused Loveday to open, and then to creep out of the room to dispatch, her hurried note.

What effect the occurrence of the morning had had upon the household generally, Loveday, in her isolated corner of the house, had no means of ascertaining. She only noted that when Hales brought in her tea, as he did precisely at five o'clock, he wore a particularly ill-tempered expression of countenance, and she heard him mutter, as he set down the tea-tray with a clatter, something about being a respectable man, and not used to such "goings on."

It was not until nearly an hour and a half after this that Mr. Craven had awakened with a sudden start, and, looking wildly around him, had questioned Loveday who had entered the room.

Loveday explained that the butler had brought in lunch at one, and tea at five, but that since then no one had come in.

"Now that's false," said Mr. Craven, in a sharp, unnatural sort of voice; "I saw him sneaking round the room, the whining, canting hypocrite, and you must have seen him, too! Didn't you hear him say, in his squeaky old voice: 'Master, I knows your secret—'" He broke off abruptly, looking wildly round. "Eh, what's this?" he cried. "No, no, I'm all wrong—Sandy is dead and buried—they held an inquest on him, and we all praised him up as if he were a saint."

"He must have been a bad man, that old Sandy," said Loveday sympathetically.

"You're right! you're right!" cried Mr. Craven, springing up excitedly from his chair and seizing her by the hand. "If ever a man deserved his death, he did. For thirty years he held that rod over my head, and then—ah where was I?"

He put his hand to his head and again sank, as if exhausted, into his chair.

"I suppose it was some early indiscretion of yours at college that he knew of?" said Loveday, eager to get at as much of the truth as possible while the mood for confidence held sway in the feeble brain.

"That was it! I was fool enough to marry a disreputable girl—a barmaid in the town—and Sandy was present at the wedding, and then—" Here his eyes closed again and his mutterings became incoherent.

For ten minutes he lay back in his chair, muttering thus; "A yelp—a groan," were the only words Loveday could distinguish among those mutterings, then suddenly, slowly and distinctly, he said, as if answering some plainly-put question: "A good blow with the hammer and the thing was done."

"I should like amazingly to see that hammer," said Loveday; "do you keep it anywhere at hand?"

His eyes opened with a wild, cunning look in them.

"Who's talking about a hammer? I did not say I had one. If anyone says I did it with a hammer, they're telling a lie."

"Oh, you've spoken to me about the hammer two or three times," said Loveday calmly; "the one that killed your dog, Captain, and I should like to see it, that's all."

The look of cunning died out of the old man's eye—"Ah, poor Captain! splendid dog that! Well, now, where were we? Where did we leave off? Ah, I remember, it was the elemental sounds of speech that bothered me so that night. Were you here then? Ah, no! I remember. I had been trying all day to assimilate a dog's yelp of pain to a human groan, and I couldn't do it. The idea haunted me—followed me about wherever I went. If they were both elemental sounds, they must have something in common, but the link between them I could not find; then it occurred to me, would a well-bred, well-trained dog like my Captain in the stables, there, at the moment of death give an unmitigated currish yelp; would there not be something of a human note in his death-cry? The thing was worth putting to the test. If I could hand down in my treatise a fragment of fact on the matter, it would be worth a dozen dogs' lives. so I went out into the moonlight—ah, but you know all about it—now, don't you?"

"Yes. Poor Captain! did he yelp or groan?"

"Why, he gave one loud, long, hideous yelp, just as if he had been a common cur. I might just as well have let him alone; it only set that other brute opening his window and spying out on me, and saying in his cracked old voice: 'Master, what are you doing out here at this time of night?'"

Again he sank back in his chair, muttering incoherently with half-closed eyes.

Loveday let him alone for a minute or so; then she had another question to ask.

"And that other brute—did he yelp or groan when you dealt him his blow?"

"What, old Sandy—the brute? he fell back—Ah, I remember, you said you would like to see the hammer that stopped his babbling old tongue—now didn't you?"

He rose a little unsteadily from his chair, and seemed to drag his long limbs with an effort across the room to a cabinet at the farther end. Opening a drawer in this cabinet, he produced, from amidst some specimens of strata and fossils, a large-sized geological hammer.

He brandished it for a moment over his head, then paused with his finger on his lip.

"Hush!" he said, "we shall have the fools creeping in to peep at us if we don't take care." And to Loveday's horror he suddenly made for the door, turned the key in the lock, withdrew it and put it into his pocket.

She looked at the clock; the hands pointed to half-past seven. Had Griffiths received her note at the proper time, and were the men now in the grounds? She could only pray that they were.

"The light is too strong for my eyes," she said, and rising from her chair, she lifted the green-shaded lamp and placed it on a table that stood at the window.

"No, no, that won't do," said Mr. Craven; "that would show everyone outside what we're doing in here." He crossed to the window as he spoke and removed the lamp thence to the mantelpiece.

Loveday could only hope that in the few seconds it had remained in the window it had caught the eye of the outside watchers.

The old man beckoned to Loveday to come near and examine his deadly weapon. "Give it a good swing round," he said, suiting the action to the word, "and down it comes with a splendid crash." He brought the hammer round within an inch of Loveday's forehead.

She started back.

"Ha, ha," he laughed harshly and unnaturally, with the light of madness dancing in his eyes now; "did I frighten you? I wonder what sort of sound you would make if I were to give you a little tap just there." Here he lightly touched her forehead with the hammer. "Elemental, of course, it would be, and—"

Loveday steadied her nerves with difficulty. Locked in with this lunatic, her only chance lay in gaining time for the detectives to reach the house and enter through the window.

"Wait a minute," she said, striving to divert his attention; "you have not yet told me what sort of an elemental sound old Sandy made when he fell. If you'll give me pen and ink, I'll write down a full account of it all, and you can incorporate it afterwards in your treatise."

For a moment a look of real pleasure flitted across the old man's face, then it faded. "The brute fell back dead without a sound," he answered; "it was all for nothing, that night's work; yet not altogether for nothing. No, I don't mind owning I would do it all over again to get the wild thrill of joy at my heart that I had when I looked down into that old man's dead face and felt myself free at last! Free at last!" his voice rang out excitedly—once more he brought his hammer round with an ugly swing.

"For a moment I was a young man again; I leaped into his room—the moon was shining full in through the window—I thought of my old college days, and the fun we used to have at Pembroke—topsy turvey I turned everything—" He broke off abruptly, and drew a step nearer to Loveday. "The pity of it all was," he said, suddenly dropping from his high, excited tone to a low, pathetic one, "that he fell without a sound of any sort." Here he drew another step nearer. "I wonder—" he said, then broke off again, and came close to Loveday's side. "It has only this moment occurred to me," he said, now with his lips close to Loveday's ear, "that a woman, in her death agony, would be much more likely to give utterance to an elemental sound than a man."

He raised his hammer, and Loveday fled to the window, and was lifted from the outside by three pairs of strong arms.

"I THOUGHT I WAS CONDUCTING my very last case—I never had such a narrow escape before!" said Loveday, as she stood talking with Mr. Griffiths on the Grenfell platform, awaiting the train to carry her back to London. "It seems strange that no one before suspected the old gentleman's sanity—I suppose, however, people were so used to his eccentricities that they did not notice how they had deepened into positive lunacy. His cunning evidently stood him in good stead at the inquest."

"It is possible" said Griffiths thoughtfully, "that he did not absolutely cross the very slender line that divided eccentricity from madness until after the murder. The excitement consequent upon the discovery of the crime may just have pushed him over the border. Now, Miss Brooke, we have exactly ten minutes before your train comes in. I should feel greatly obliged to you if you would explain one or two things that have a professional interest for me."

"With pleasure," said Loveday. "Put your questions in categorical order and I will answer them."

"Well, then, in the first place, what suggested to your mind the old man's guilt?"

"The relations that subsisted between him and Sandy seemed to me to savour too much of fear on the one side and power on the other. Also the income paid to Sandy during Mr. Craven's absence in Natal bore, to my mind, an unpleasant resemblance to hush-money."

"Poor wretched being! And I hear that, after all, the woman he married in his wild young days died soon afterwards of drink. I have no doubt, however, that Sandy sedulously kept up the fiction of her existence, even after his master's second marriage. Now for another question: how was it you knew that Miss Craven had taken her brother's place in the sick-room?"

"On the evening of my arrival I discovered a rather long lock of fair hair in the unswept fireplace of my room, which, as it happened, was usually occupied by Miss Craven. It at once occurred to me that the young lady had been cutting off her hair and that there must be some powerful motive to induce such a sacrifice. The suspicious circumstances attending her brother's illness soon supplied me with such a motive."

"Ah! that typhoid fever business was very cleverly done. Not a servant in the house, I verily believe, but who thought Master Harry was upstairs, ill in bed, and Miss Craven away at her friends' in Newcastle. The young fellow must have got a clear start off within an hour of the murder. His sister, sent away the next day to Newcastle, dismissed her maid there, I hear, on the plea of no accommodation at her friends' house—sent the girl to her own home for a holiday and herself returned to Troyte's Hill in the middle of the night, having walked the five miles from Grenfell. No doubt her mother admitted her through one of those easily-opened front windows, cut her hair and put her to bed to personate her brother without delay. With Miss Craven's strong likeness to Master Harry, and in a darkened room, it is easy to understand that the eyes of a doctor, personally unacquainted with the family, might easily be deceived. Now, Miss Brooke, you must admit that with all this elaborate chicanery and double dealing going on, it was only natural that my suspicions should set in strongly in that quarter."

"I read it all in another light, you see," said Loveday. "It seemed to me that the mother, knowing her son's evil proclivities, believed in his guilt, in spite, possibly, of his assertions of innocence. The son, most likely, on his way back to the house after pledging the family plate, had met old Mr. Craven with the hammer in his hand. Seeing, no doubt, how impossible it would be for him to clear himself without incriminating his father, he preferred flight to Natal to giving evidence at the inquest."

"Now about his alias?" said Mr. Griffiths briskly, for the train was at that moment steaming into the station. "How did you know that Harold Cousins was identical with Harry Craven, and had sailed in the *Bonnie Dundee*?"

"Oh, that was easy enough," said Loveday, as she stepped into the train; "a newspaper sent down to Mr. Craven by his wife, was folded so as to direct his attention to the shipping list. In it I saw that the *Bonnie Dundee* had sailed two days previously for Natal. Now it was only natural to connect Natal with Mrs. Craven, who had passed the greater part of her life there; and it was easy to understand her wish to get her scapegrace son among her early friends. The alias under which he sailed came readily enough to light. I found it scribbled all over one of Mr. Craven's writing pads in his study; evidently it had been drummed into his ears by his wife as his son's alias, and the old gentleman had taken this method of fixing it in his memory. We'll hope that the young fellow, under his new name, will make a new reputation for himself—at any rate, he'll have a better chance of doing so with the ocean between him and his evil companions. Now it's good-bye, I think."

"No," said Mr. Griffiths; "it's au revoir, for you'll have to come back again for the assizes, and give the evidence that will shut old Mr. Craven in an asylum for the rest of his life."

THE REDHILL SISTERHOOD

They want you at Redhill, now," said Mr. Dyer, taking a packet of papers from one of his pigeon-holes. "The idea seems gaining ground in manly quarters that in cases of mere suspicion, women detectives are more satisfactory than men, for they are less likely to attract attention. And this Redhill affair, so far as I can make out, is one of suspicion only."

It was a dreary November morning; every gas jet in the Lynch Court office was alight, and a yellow curtain of outside fog draped its narrow windows.

"Nevertheless, I suppose one can't afford to leave it uninvestigated at this season of the year, with country-house robberies beginning in so many quarters," said Miss Brooke.

"No; and the circumstances in this case certainly seem to point in the direction of the country-house burglar. Two days ago a somewhat curious application was made privately, by a man giving the name of John Murray, to Inspector Gunning, of the Reigate police—Redhill, I must tell you is in the Reigate police district. Murray stated that he had been a greengrocer somewhere in South London, had sold his business there, and had, with the proceeds of the sale, bought two small houses in Redhill, intending to let the one and live in the other. These houses are situated in a blind alley, known as Paved Court, a narrow turning leading off the London and Brighton coach road. Paved Court has been known to the sanitary authorities for the past ten years as a regular fever nest, and as the houses which Murray bought—numbers 7 and 8—stand at the very end of the blind alley, with no chance of thorough ventilation, I dare say the man got them for next to nothing. He told the Inspector that he had had great difficulty in procuring a tenant for the house he wished to let, number 8, and that consequently when, about three weeks back, a lady, dressed as a nun, made him an offer for it, he immediately closed with her. The lady gave her name simply as 'Sister Monica,' and stated that she was a member of an undenominational Sisterhood that had recently been founded by a wealthy lady, who wished her name kept a secret. Sister Monica gave no references, but, instead, paid a quarter's rent in advance, saying that she wished to take possession of the house immediately, and open it as a home for crippled orphans."

"Gave no references—home for cripples," murmured Loveday, scribbling hard and fast in her note-book.

"Murray made no objection to this," continued Mr. Dyer, "and, accordingly, the next day, Sister Monica, accompanied by three other Sisters and some sickly children, took possession of the house, which they furnished with the barest possible necessaries from cheap shops in the neighbourhood. For a time, Murray said, he thought he had secured most desirable tenants, but during the last ten days suspicions as to their real character have entered his mind, and these suspicions he thought it his duty to communicate to the police. Among their possessions, it seems, these Sisters number an old donkey and a tiny cart, and this they start daily on a sort of begging tour through the adjoining villages, bringing back every evening a perfect hoard of broken victuals and bundles of old garments. Now comes the extraordinary fact on which Murray bases his suspicions. He says, and Gunning verifies his statement, that in whatever direction those Sisters turn the wheels of their donkey-cart, burglaries, or attempts at burglaries, are sure to follow. A week ago they went along towards Horley, where, at an outlying house, they received much kindness from a wealthy gentleman. That very night an attempt was made to break into that gentleman's house—an attempt, however, that was happily frustrated by the barking of the house-dog. And so on in other instances that I need not go into. Murray suggests that it might be as well to have the daily movements of these sisters closely watched, and that extra vigilance should be exercised by the police in the districts that have had the honour of a morning call from them. Gunning coincides with this idea, and so has sent to me to secure your services."

Loveday closed her note-book. "I suppose Gunning will meet me somewhere and tell me where I'm to take up my quarters?" she said.

"Yes; he will get into your carriage at Merstham—the station before Redhill—if you will put your hand out of window, with the morning paper in it. By-the-way, he takes it for granted that you will save the 11.5 train from Victoria. Murray, it seems has been good enough to place his little house at the disposal of the police, but Gunning does not think espionage could be so well carried on there as from other quarters. The presence of a stranger in an alley of that sort is bound to attract attention. So he has hired a room for you in a draper's shop that immediately faces the head of the court. There is a private door to this shop of which you will have the key, and can let yourself in and out as you please. You are supposed to be a nursery governess on the lookout for a situation, and Gunning will keep you supplied with letters to give colour to the idea. He suggests that you need only occupy the room during the day, at night you will find far more comfortable quarters at Laker's Hotel, just outside the town."

This was about the sum total of the instructions that Mr. Dyer had to give.

The 11.5 train from Victoria, that carried Loveday to her work among the Surrey Hills, did not get clear of the London fog till well away on the other side of Purley. When the train halted at Merstham, in response to her signal a tall, soldier-like individual made for her carriage, and, jumping in, took the seat facing her. He introduced himself to her as Inspector Gunning, recalled to her memory a former occasion on which they had met, and then, naturally enough, turned the talk upon the present suspicious circumstances they were bent upon investigating.

"It won't do for you and me to be seen together," he said; "of course I am known for miles round, and anyone seen in my company will be at once set down as my coadjutor, and spied upon accordingly. I walked from Redhill to Merstham on purpose to avoid recognition on the platform at Redhill, and half-way here, to my great annoyance, found that I was being followed by a man in a workman's dress and carrying a basket of tools. I doubled, however, and gave him the slip, taking a short cut down a lane which, if he had been living in the place, he would have known as well as I did. By Jove!" this was added with a sudden start, "there is the fellow, I declare; he has weathered me after all, and has no doubt taken good stock of us both, with the train going at this snail's pace. It was unfortunate that your face should have been turned towards that window, Miss Brooke."

"My veil is something of a disguise, and I will put on another cloak before he has a chance of seeing me again," said Loveday.

All she had seen in the brief glimpse that the train had allowed, was a tall, powerfully-built man walking along a siding of the line. His cap was drawn low over his eyes, and in his hand he carried a workman's basket.

Gunning seemed much annoyed at the circumstance. "Instead of landing at Redhill," he said, "we'll go on to Three Bridges and wait there for a Brighton train to bring us back, that will enable you to get to your room somewhere between the lights; I don't want to have you spotted before you've so much as started your work."

Then they went back to their discussion of the Redhill Sisterhood.

"They call themselves 'undenominational,' whatever that means," said Gunning "they say they are connected with no religious sect whatever, they attend sometimes one place of worship, sometimes another, sometimes none at all. They refuse to give up the name of the founder of their order, and really no one has any right to demand it of them, for, as no doubt you see, up to the present moment the case is one of mere suspicion, and it may be a pure coincidence that attempts at burglary have followed their footsteps in this neighbourhood. By-the-way, I have heard of a man's face being enough to hang him, but until I saw Sister Monica's, I never saw a woman's face that could perform the same kind office for her. Of all the lowest criminal types of faces I have ever seen, I think hers is about the lowest and most repulsive."

After the Sisters, they passed in review the chief families resident in the neighbourhood.

"This," said Gunning, unfolding a paper, "is a map I have specially drawn up for you—it takes in the district for ten miles round Redhill, and every country house of any importance is marked with it in red ink. Here, in addition, is an index to those houses, with special notes of my own to every house."

Loveday studied the map for a minute or so, then turned her attention to the index.

"Those four houses you've marked, I see, are those that have been already attempted. I don't think I'll run them through, but I'll mark them 'doubtful;' you see the gang—for, of course, it is a gang—might follow our reasoning on the matter, and look upon those houses as our weak point. Here's one I'll run through, 'house empty during winter months,' that means plate and jewellery sent to the bankers. Oh! and this one may as well be crossed off, 'father and four sons all athletes and sportsmen,' that means firearms always handy—I don't think burglars will be likely to trouble them. Ah! now we come to something! Here's a house to be marked 'tempting' in a burglar's list. 'Wootton Hall, lately changed hands and re-built, with complicated passages and corridors. Splendid family plate in daily use and left entirely to the care of the butler.' I wonder, does the master of that house trust to his 'complicated passages' to preserve his plate for him? A dismissed dishonest servant would supply a dozen maps of the place for half-a-sovereign. What do these initials, 'E.L.,' against the next house in the list, North Cape, stand for?"

"Electric lighted. I think you might almost cross that house off also. I consider electric lighting one of the greatest safeguards against burglars that a man can give his house."

"Yes, if he doesn't rely exclusively upon it; it might be a nasty trap under certain circumstances. I see this gentleman also has magnificent presentation and other plate."

"Yes. Mr. Jameson is a wealthy man and very popular in the neighbourhood; his cups and epergnes are worth looking at."

"Is it the only house in the district that is lighted with electricity?"

"Yes; and, begging your pardon, Miss Brooke, I only wish it were not so. If electric lighting were generally in vogue it would save the police a lot of trouble on these dark winter nights."

"The burglars would find some way of meeting such a condition of things, depend upon it; they have reached a very high development in these days. They no longer stalk about as they did fifty years ago with blunderbuss and bludgeon; they plot, plan, contrive and bring imagination and artistic resource to their aid. By-the-way, it often occurs to me that the popular detective stories, for which there seems to large a demand at the present day, must be, at times, uncommonly useful to the criminal classes."

At Three Bridges they had to wait so long for a return train that it was nearly dark when Loveday got back to Redhill. Mr. Gunning did not accompany her thither, having alighted at a previous station. Loveday had directed her portmanteau to be sent direct to Laker's Hotel, where she had engaged a room by telegram from Victoria Station. So, unburthened by luggage, she slipped quietly out of the Redhill Station and made her way straight for the draper's shop in the London Road. She had no difficulty in finding it, thanks to the minute directions given her by the Inspector.

Street lamps were being lighted in the sleepy little town as she went along, and as she turned into the London Road, shopkeepers were lighting up their windows on both sides of the way. A few yards down this road, a dark patch between the lighted shops showed her where Paved Court led off from the thoroughfare. A side-door of one of the shops that stood at the corner of the court seemed to offer a post of observation whence she could see without being seen, and here Loveday, shrinking into the shadows, ensconced herself in order to take stock of the little alley and its inhabitants. She found it much as it had been described to her—a collection of four-roomed houses of which more than half were unlet. Numbers 7 and 8 at the head of the court presented a slightly less neglected appearance than the other tenements. Number 7 stood in total darkness, but in the upper window of number 8 there showed what seemed to be a night-light burning, so Loveday conjectured that this possibly was the room set apart as a dormitory for the little cripples.

While she stood thus surveying the home of the suspected Sisterhood, the Sisters themselves—two, at least, of them—came into view, with their donkey-cart and their cripples, in the main road. It was an odd little cortège. One Sister, habited in a nun's dress of dark blue serge, led the donkey by the bridle; another Sister, similarly attired, walked alongside the low cart, in which were seated two sickly-looking children. They were evidently returning from one of their long country circuits, and unless they had lost their way and been belated—it certainly seemed a late hour for the sickly little cripples to be abroad.

As they passed under the gas lamp at the corner of the court, Loveday caught a glimpse of the faces of the Sisters. It was easy, with Inspector Gunning's description before her mind, to identify the older and taller woman as Sister Monica, and a more coarse-featured and generally repellant face Loveday admitted to herself she had never before seen. In striking contrast to this forbidding countenance, was that of the younger Sister. Loveday could only catch a brief passing view of it, but that one brief view was enough to impress it on her memory as of unusual sadness and beauty. As the donkey stopped at the corner of the court, Loveday heard this sad-looking young woman addressed as "Sister Anna" by one of the cripples, who asked plaintively when they were going to have something to eat.

"Now, at once," said Sister Anna, lifting the little one, as it seemed to Loveday, tenderly out of the cart, and carrying him on her shoulder down the court to the door of number 8, which opened to them at their approach. The other Sister did the same with the other child; then both Sisters returned, unloaded the cart of sundry bundles and baskets, and, this done, led off the old donkey and trap down the road, possibly to a neighbouring costermonger's stables.

A man, coming along on a bicycle, exchanged a word of greeting with the Sisters as they passed, then swung himself off his machine at the corner of the court, and walked it along the paved way to the door of number 7. This he opened with a key, and then, pushing the machine before him, entered the house.

Loveday took it for granted that this man must be the John Murray of whom she had heard. She had closely scrutinized him as he had passed her, and had seen that he was a dark, well-featured man of about fifty years of age.

She congratulated herself on her good fortune in having seen so much in such a brief space of time, and coming forth from her sheltered corner turned her steps in the direction of the draper's shop on the other side of the road.

It was easy to find it. "Golightly" was the singular name that figured above the shop-front, in which were displayed a variety of goods calculated to meet the wants of servants and the poorer classes generally. A tall, powerfully-built man appeared to be looking in at this window. Loveday's foot was on the doorstep of the draper's private entrance, her hand on the door-knocker, when this individual, suddenly turning, convinced her of his identity with the journeyman workman who had so disturbed Mr. Gunning's equanimity. It was true he wore a bowler instead of a journeyman's cap, and he no longer carried a basket of tools, but there was no possibility for anyone, with so good an eye for an outline as Loveday possessed, not to recognize the carriage of the head and shoulders as that of the man she had seen walking along the railway siding. He gave her no time to make minute observation of his appearance, but turned quickly away, and disappeared down a by-street.

Loveday's work seemed to bristle with difficulties now. Here was she, as it were, unearthed in her own ambush; for there could be but little doubt that during the whole time she had stood watching those Sisters, that man, from a safe vantage point, had been watching her.

She found Mrs. Golightly a civil and obliging person. She showed Loveday to her room above the shop, brought her the letters which Inspector Gunning had been careful to have posted to her during the day. Then she supplied her with pen and ink and, in response to Loveday's request, with some strong coffee that she said, with a little attempt at a joke, would "keep a dormouse awake all through the winter without winking."

While the obliging landlady busied herself about the room, Loveday had a few questions to ask about the Sisterhood who lived down the court opposite. On this head, however, Mrs. Golightly could tell her no more than she already knew, beyond the fact that they started every morning on their rounds at eleven o'clock punctually, and that before that hour they were never to be seen outside their door.

Loveday's watch that night was to be a fruitless one. Although she sat, with her lamp turned out and safely screened from observation, until close upon midnight, with eyes fixed upon numbers 7 and 8 Paved Court, not so much as a door opening or shutting at either house rewarded her vigil. The lights flitted from the lower to the upper floors in both houses, and then disappeared somewhere between nine and ten in the evening; and after that, not a sign of life did either tenement show.

And all through the long hours of that watch, backwards and forwards there seemed to flit before her mind's eye, as if in some sort it were fixed upon its retina, the sweet, sad face of Sister Anna.

Why it was this face should so haunt her, she found it hard to say.

"It has a mournful past and a mournful future written upon it as a hopeless whole," she said to herself. "It is the face of an Andromeda! 'here am I,' it seems to say, 'tied to my stake, helpless and hopeless.'"

The church clocks were sounding the midnight hour as Loveday made her way through the dark streets to her hotel outside the town. As she passed under the railway arch that ended in the open country road, the echo of not very distant footsteps caught her ear. When she stopped they stopped, when she went on they went on, and she knew that once more she was being followed and watched, although the darkness of the arch prevented her seeing even the shadow of the man who was thus dogging her steps.

The next morning broke keen and frosty. Loveday studied her map and her country-house index over a seven o'clock breakfast, and then set off for a brisk walk along the country road. No doubt in London the streets were walled in and roofed with yellow fog; here, however, bright sunshine played in and out of the bare tree-boughs and leafless hedges on to a thousand frost spangles, turning the prosaic macadamized road into a gangway fit for Queen Titania herself and her fairy train.

Loveday turned her back on the town and set herself to follow the road as it wound away over the hill in the direction of a village called Northfield. Early as she was, she was not to have that road to herself. A team of strong horses trudged by on their way to their work in the fuller's-earth pits. A young fellow on a bicycle flashed past at a tremendous pace, considering the upward slant of the road. He looked hard at her as he passed, then slackened pace, dismounted, and awaited her coming on the brow of the hill.

"Good morning, Miss Brooke," he said, lifting his cap as she came alongside of him. "May I have five minutes' talk with you?"

The young man who thus accosted her had not the appearance of a gentleman. He was a handsome, bright-faced young fellow of about two-and-twenty, and was dressed in ordinary cyclists' dress; his cap was pushed back from his brow over thick, curly, fair hair, and Loveday, as she looked at him, could not repress the thought how well he would look at the head of a troop of cavalry, giving the order to charge the enemy.

He led his machine to the side of the footpath.

"You have the advantage of me," said Loveday; "I haven't the remotest notion who you are."

"No," he said; "although I know you, you cannot possibly know me. I am a north country man, and I was present, about a month ago, at the trial of old Mr. Craven, of Troyte's Hill—in fact, I acted as reporter for one of the local papers. I watched your face so closely as you gave your evidence that I should know it anywhere, among a thousand."

"And your name is—?"

"George White, of Grenfell. My father is part proprietor of one of the Newcastle papers. I am a bit of a literary man myself, and sometimes figure as a reporter, sometimes as leader-writer, to that paper." Here he gave a glance towards his side pocket, from which protruded a small volume of Tennyson's poems.

The facts he had stated did not seem to invite comment, and Loveday exclaimed merely:

"Indeed!"

The young man went back to the subject that was evidently filling his thoughts. "I have special reasons for being glad to have met you this morning, Miss Brooke," he want on, making his footsteps keep pace with hers. "I am in great trouble, and I believe you are the only person in the whole world who can help me out of that trouble."

"I am rather doubtful as to my power of helping anyone out of trouble," said Loveday; "so far as my experience goes, our troubles are as much a part of ourselves as our skins are of our bodies."

"Ah, but not such trouble as mine," said White eagerly. He broke off for a moment, then, with a sudden rush of words, told her what that trouble was. For the past year he had been engaged to be married to a young girl, who, until quite recently had been fulfilling the duties of a nursery governess in a large house in the neighbourhood of Redhill.

"Will you kindly give me the name of that house?" interrupted Loveday.

"Certainly; Wootton Hall, the place is called, and Annie Lee is my sweetheart's name. I don't care who knows it!" He threw his head back as he said this, as if he would be delighted to announce the fact to the whole world. "Annie's mother," he went on, "died when she was a baby, and we both thought her father was dead also, when suddenly, about a fortnight ago, it came to her knowledge that instead of being dead, he was serving his time at Portland for some offence committed years ago."

"Do you know how this came to Annie's knowledge?"

"Not the least in the world; I only know that I suddenly got a letter from her announcing the fact, and at the same time, breaking off her engagement with me. I tore the letter into a thousand pieces, and wrote back saying I would not allow the engagement to be broken off, but would marry her to-morrow if she would have me. To this letter she did not reply; there came instead a few lines from Mrs. Copeland, the lady at Wootton Hall, saying that Annie had thrown up her engagement and joined some Sisterhood, and that she, Mrs. Copeland, had pledged her word to Annie to reveal to no one the name and whereabouts of that Sisterhood."

"And I suppose you imagine I am able to do what Mrs. Copeland is pledged not to do?"

"That's just it, Miss Brooke," cried the young man enthusiastically. "You do such wonderful things; everyone knows you do. It seems as if, when anything is wanted to be found out, you just walk into a place, look round you and, in a moment, everything becomes clear as noonday."

"I can't quite lay claim to such wonderful powers as that. As it happens, however, in the present instance, no particular skill is needed to find out what you wish to know, for I fancy I have already come upon the traces of Miss Annie Lee."

"Miss Brooke!"

"Of course, I cannot say for certain, but is a matter you can easily settle for yourself—settle, too, in a way that will confer a great obligation on me."

"I shall be only too delighted to be of any—the slightest service to you," cried White, enthusiastically as before.

"Thank you. I will explain. I came down here specially to watch the movements of a certain Sisterhood who have somehow aroused the suspicions of the police. Well, I find that instead of being able to do this, I am myself so closely watched—possibly by confederates of these

Sisters—that unless I can do my work by deputy I may as well go back to town at once."

"Ah! I see—you want me to be that deputy."

"Precisely. I want you to go to the room in Redhill that I have hired, take your place at the window—screened, of course, from observation—at which I ought to be seated—watch as closely as possible the movements of these Sisters and report them to me at the hotel, where I shall remain shut in from morning till night—it is the only way in which I can throw my persistent spies off the scent. Now, in doing this for me, you will be also doing yourself a good turn, for I have little doubt but what under the blue serge hood of one of the sisters you will discover the pretty face of Miss Annie Lee."

As they had talked they had walked, and now stood on the top of the hill at the head of the one little street that constituted the whole of the village of Northfield.

On their left hand stood the village schools and the master's house; nearly facing these, on the opposite side of the road, beneath a clump of elms, stood the village pound. Beyond this pound, on either side of the way, were two rows of small cottages with tiny squares of garden in front, and in the midst of these small cottages a swinging sign beneath a lamp announced a "Postal and Telegraph Office."

"Now that we have come into the land of habitations again," said Loveday, "it will be best for us to part. It will not do for you and me to be seen together, or my spies will be transferring their attentions from me to you, and I shall have to find another deputy. You had better start on your bicycle for Redhill at once, and I will walk back at leisurely speed. Come to me at my hotel without fail at one o'clock and report proceedings. I do not say anything definite about remuneration, but I assure you, if you carry out my instructions to the letter, your services will be amply rewarded by me and by my employers."

There were yet a few more details to arrange. White had been, he said, only a day and night in the neighbourhood, and special directions as to the locality had to be given to him. Loveday advised him not to attract attention by going to the draper's private door, but to enter the shop as if he were a customer, and then explain matters to Mrs. Golightly, who, no doubt, would be in her place behind the counter; tell her he was the brother of the Miss Smith who had hired her room, and ask permission to go through the shop to that room, as he had been commissioned by his sister to read and answer any letters that might have arrived there for her.

"Show her the key of the side door—here it is," said Loveday; "it will be your credentials, and tell her you did not like to make use of it without acquainting her with the fact."

The young man took the key, endeavoured to put it in his waistcoat pocket, found the space there occupied and so transferred it to the keeping of a side pocket in his tunic.

All this time Loveday stood watching him.

"You have a capital machine there," she said, as the young man mounted his bicycle once more, "and I hope you will turn it to account in following the movements of these Sisters about the neighbourood. I feel confident you will have something definite to tell me when you bring me your first report at one o'clock."

White once more broke into a profusion of thanks, and then, lifting his cap to the lady, started his machine at a fairly good pace.

Loveday watched him out of sight down the slope of the hill, then, instead of following him as she had said she would "at a leisurely pace," she turned her steps in the opposite direction along the village street.

It was an altogether ideal country village. Neatly-dressed chubby-faced children, now on their way to the schools, dropped quaint little curtsies, or tugged at curly locks as Loveday passed; every cottage looked the picture of cleanliness and trimness, and although so late in the year, the gardens were full of late flowering chrysanthemums and early flowering Christmas roses.

At the end of the village, Loveday came suddenly into view of a large, handsome, red-brick mansion. It presented a wide frontage to the road, from which it lay back amid extensive pleasure grounds. On the right hand, and a little in the rear of the house, stood what seemed to be large and commodious stables, and immediately adjoining these stables was a low-built, red-brick shed, that had evidently been recently erected.

That low-build, red-brick shed excited Loveday's curiosity.

"Is this house called North Cape?" she asked of a man, who chanced at that moment to be passing with a pickaxe and shovel.

The man answered in the affirmative, and Loveday then asked another question: could he tell her what was that small shed so close to the house—it looked like a glorified cowhouse—now what could be its use?

The man's face lighted up as if it were a subject on which he liked to be questioned. He explained that that small shed was the engine-house where the electricity that lighted North Cape was made and stored. Then he dwelt with pride upon the fact, as if he held a personal interest in it, that North Cape was the only house, far or near, that was thus lighted.

"I suppose the wires are carried underground to the house," said Loveday, looking in vain for signs of them anywhere.

The man was delighted to go into details on the matter. He had helped to lay those wires, he said: they were two in number, one for supply and one for return, and were laid three feet below ground, in boxes filled with pitch. These wires were switched on to jars in the engine-house, where the electricity was stored, and, after passing underground, entered the family mansion under its flooring at its western end.

Loveday listened attentively to these details, and then took a minute and leisurely survey of the house and its surroundings. This done, she retraced her steps through the village, pausing, however, at the "Postal and Telegraph Office" to dispatch a telegram to Inspector Gunning.

It was one to send the Inspector to his cipher-book. It ran as follows:

"Rely solely on chemist and coal-merchant throughout the day.—L. B."

After this, she quickened her pace, and in something over three-quarters of an hour was back again at her hotel.

There she found more of life stirring than when she had quitted it in the early morning. There was to be a meeting of the "Surrey Stags," about a couple of miles off, and a good many hunting men were hanging about the entrance to the house, discussing the chances of sport after last night's frost. Loveday made her way through the throng in leisurely fashion, and not a man but what had keen scrutiny from her sharp eyes. No, there was no cause for suspicion there: they were evidently one and all just what they seemed to be—loud-voiced, hard-riding men, bent on a day's sport; but—and here Loveday's eyes traveled beyond the hotel court-yard to the other side of the road—who was that man with a bill-hook hacking at the hedge there—a thin-featured, round-shouldered old fellow, with a bent-about hat? It might be as well not to take it too rashly for granted that her spies had withdrawn, and had left her free to do her work in her own fashion.

She went upstairs to her room. It was situated on the first floor in the front of the house, and consequently commanded a good view of the high road. She stood well back from the window, and at an angle whence she could see and not be seen, took a long, steady survey of the hedger. And the longer she looked the more convinced she was that the man's real work was something other than the bill-hook seemed to imply. He worked, so to speak, with his head over his shoulder, and when Loveday supplemented her eyesight with a strong field-glass, she could see more than one stealthy glance shot from beneath his bent-about hat in the direction of her window.

There could be little doubt about it: her movements were to be as closely watched to-day as they had been yesterday. Now it was of first importance that she should communicate with Inspector Gunning in the course of the afternoon: the question to solve was how it was to be done?

To all appearance Loveday answered the question in extraordinary fashion. She pulled up her blind, she drew back her curtain, and seated herself, in full view, at a small table in the window recess. Then she took a pocket inkstand from her pocket, a packet or correspondence cards from her letter-case, and with rapid pen, set to work on them.

About an hour and a half afterwards, White, coming in, according to his promise, to report proceedings, found her still seated at the window, not, however, with writing materials before her, but with needle and thread in her hand with which she was mending her gloves.

"I return to town by the first train to-morrow morning," she said as he entered, "and I find these wretched things want no end of stitches. Now for your report."

White appeared to be in an elated frame of mind. "I've seen her!" he cried, "my Annie—they've got her, those confounded Sisters; but they sha'n't keep her—no, not if I have to pull the house down about their ears to get her out."

"Well, now you know where she is, you can take your time about getting her out," said Loveday. "I hope, however, you haven't broken faith with me, and betrayed yourself by trying to speak with her, because, if so, I shall have to look out for another deputy."

"Honour, Miss Brooke!" answered White indignantly. "I stuck to my duty, though it cost me something to see her hanging over those kids and tucking them into the cart, and never say a word to her, never so much as wave my hand."

"Did she go out with the donkey-cart to-day?"

"No, she only tucked the kids into the cart with a blanket, and then went back to the house. Two old Sisters, ugly as sin, went out with them. I watched them from the window, jolt, jolt, jolt, round the corner,

CATHERINE LOUISA PIRKIS

out of sight, and then I whipped down the stairs, and on to my machine, and was after them in a trice and managed to keep them well in sight for over an hour and a half."

"And their destination to-day was?"

"Wootton Hall."

"Ah, just as I expected."

"Just as you expected?" echoed White.

"I forgot. You do not know the nature of the suspicions that are attached to this Sisterhood, and the reasons I have for thinking that Wootton Hall, at this season of the year, might have an especial attraction for them."

White continued staring at her. "Miss Brooke," he said presently, in an altered tone, "whatever suspicions may attach to the Sisterhood, I'll stake my life on it, my Annie has had no share in any wickedness of any sort."

"Oh, quite so; it is most likely that your Annie has, in some way, been inveigled into joining these Sisters—has been taken possession of by them, in fact, just as they have taken possession of the little cripples."

"That's it!" he cried excitedly; "that was the idea that occurred to me when you spoke to me on the hill about them, otherwise you may be sure—"

"Did they get relief of any sort at the Hall?" interrupted Loveday.

"Yes; one of the two ugly old women stopped outside the lodge gates with the donkey-cart, and the other beauty went up to the house alone. She stayed there, I should think, about a quarter of an hour, and when she came back, was followed by a servant, carrying a bundle and a basket."

"Ah! I've no doubt they brought away with them something else beside old garments and broken victuals."

White stood in front of her, fixing a hard, steady gaze upon her.

"Miss Brooke," he said presently, in a voice that matched the look on his face, "what do you suppose was the real object of these women in going to Wootton Hall this morning?"

"Mr. White, if I wished to help a gang of thieves break into Wootton Hall tonight, don't you think I should be greatly interested in procuring from them the information that the master of the house was away from home; that two of the men servants, who slept in the house, had recently been dismissed and their places had not yet been filled; also that the dogs were never unchained at night, and that their kennels were at the side of the house at which the butler's pantry is not situated? These are particulars I have gathered in this house without stirring from my chair, and I am satisfied that they are likely to be true. A the same time, if I were a professed burglar, I should not be content with information that was likely to be true, but would be careful to procure such that was certain to be true, and so would set accomplices to work at the fountain head. Now do you understand?"

White folded his arms and looked down on her.

"What are you going to do?" he asked, in short, brusque tones.

Loveday looked him full in the face. "Communicate with the police immediately," she answered; "and I should feel greatly obliged if you will at once take a note from me to Inspector Gunning at Reigate."

"And what becomes of Annie?"

"I don't think you need have any anxiety on that head. I've no doubt that when the circumstances of her admission to the Sisterhood are investigated, it will be proved that she has been as much deceived and imposed upon as the man, John Murray, who so foolishly let his house to these women. Remember, Annie has Mrs. Copeland's good word to support her integrity."

White stood silent for awhile.

"What sort of a note do you wish me to take to the Inspector?" he presently asked.

"You shall read it as I write it, if you like," answered Loveday. She took a correspondence card from her letter case, and, with an indelible pencil, wrote as follows—

Wooton Hall is threatened to-night—concentrate attention there.

L. B.

White read the words as she wrote them with a curious expression passing over his handsome features.

"Yes," he said, curtly as before. "I'll deliver that, I give you my word, but I'll bring back no answer to you. I'll do no more spying for you—it's a trade that doesn't suit me. There's a straight-forward way of doing straight-forward work, and I'll take that way—no other—to get my Annie out of that den."

He took the note, which she sealed and handed to him, and strode out of the room.

Loveday, from the window, watched him mount his bicycle. Was it her fancy, or did there pass a swift, furtive glance of recognition between him and the hedger on the other side of the way as he rode out of the court-yard?

Loveday seemed determined to make that hedger's work easy for him. The short winter's day was closing in now, and her room must consequently have been growing dim to outside observation. She lighted the gas chandelier which hung from the ceiling and, still with blinds and curtains undrawn, took her old place at the window, spread writing materials before her and commenced a long and elaborate report to her chief at Lynch Court.

About half-an-hour afterwards, as she threw a casual glance across the road, she saw that the hedger had disappeared, but that two ill-looking tramps sat munching bread and cheese under the hedge to which his bill-hook had done so little service. Evidently the intention was, one way or another, not to lose sight of her so long as she remained in Redhill.

Meantime, White had delivered Loveday's note to the Inspector at Reigate, and had disappeared on his bicycle once more.

Gunning read it without a change of expression. Then he crossed the room to the fire-place and held the card as close to the bars as he could without scorching it.

"I had a telegram from her this morning," he explained to his confidential man, "telling me to rely upon chemicals and coals throughout the day, and that, of course, meant that she would write to me in invisible ink. No doubt this message about Wootton Hall means nothing—"

He broke off abruptly, exclaiming: "Eh! what's this!" as, having withdrawn the card from the fire, Loveday's real message stood out in bold, clear characters between the lines of the false one.

Thus it ran:

North Cape will be attacked to-night—a desperate gang—
be prepared for a struggle. Above all, guard the electrical
engine-house. On no account attempt to communicate with
me; I am so closely watched that any endeavour to do so may
frustrate your chance of trapping the scoundrels.

L. B.

That night when the moon went down behind Reigate Hill an exciting scene was enacted at "North Cape." The *Surrey Gazette*, in its issue the following day, gave the subjoined account of it under the heading, "Desperate encounter with burglars."

"Last night, 'North Cape,' the residence of Mr. Jameson, was the scene of an affray between the police and a desperate gang of burglars. 'North Cape' is lighted throughout with electricity, and the burglars, four in number, divided in half—two being told off to enter and rob the house, and two to remain at the engine-shed, where the electricity is stored, so that, at a given signal, should need arise, the wires might be unswitched, the inmates of the house thrown into sudden darkness and confusion, and the escape of the marauders thereby facilitated. Mr. Jameson, however, had received timely warning from the police of the intended attack, and he, with his two sons, all well armed, sat in darkness in the inner hall awaiting the coming of the thieves. The police were stationed, some in the stables, some in out-buildings nearer to the house, and others in more distant parts of the grounds. The burglars effected their entrance by means of a ladder placed to a window of the servants' stair case which leads straight down to the butler's pantry and to the safe where the silver is kept. The fellows, however, had no sooner got into the house than the police issuing from their hiding-place outside, mounted the ladder after them and thus cut off their retreat. Mr. Jameson and his two sons, at the same moment, attacked them in front, and thus overwhelmed by numbers, the scoundrels were easily secured. It was at the engine-house outside that the sharpest struggle took place. The thieves had forced open the door of this engine-shed with their jimmies immediately on their arrival, under the very eyes of the police, who lay in ambush in the stables, and when one of the men, captured in the house, contrived to sound an alarm on his whistle, these outside watchers made a rush for the electrical jars, in order to unswitch the wires. Upon this the police closed upon them, and a hand-to-hand struggle followed, and if it had not been for the timely assistance of Mr. Jameson and his sons, who had fortunately conjectured that their presence here might be useful, it is more than likely that one of the burglars, a powerfully-built man, would have escaped.

"The names of the captured men are John Murray, Arthur and George Lee (father and son), and a man with so many aliases that it is difficult to know which is his real name. The whole thing had been most cunningly and carefully planned. The elder Lee, lately released from penal servitude for a similar offence, appears to have been prime mover in the affair. This man had, it seems, a son and a daughter, who, through the kindness of friends, had been fairly well placed in life: the son at an electrical engineers' in London, the daughter as nursery governess at Wootton Hall. Directly this man was released from Portland, he seems to have found out his children and done his best to ruin them both. He was constantly at Wootton Hall endeavouring to induce his daughter to act as an accomplice to a robbery of the house. This so worried the girl that she threw up her situation and joined a Sisterhood that had recently been established in the neighbourhood. Upon this, Lee's thoughts turned in another direction. He induced his son, who had saved a little money, to throw up his work in London, and join him in his disreputable career. The boy is a handsome young fellow, but appears to have in him the makings of a first-class criminal. In his work as an electrical engineer he had made the acquaintance of the man John Murray, who, it is said, has been rapidly going downhill of late. Murray was the owner of the house rented by the Sisterhood that Miss Lee had joined, and the idea evidently struck the brains of these three scoundrels that this Sisterhood, whose antecedents were a little mysterious, might be utilized to draw off the attention of the police from themselves and from the especial house in the neighbourhood that they had planned to attack. With this end in view, Murray made an application to the police to have the Sisters watched, and still further to give colour to the suspicions he had endeavoured to set afloat concerning them, he and his confederates made feeble attempts at burglary upon the houses at which the Sisters had called, begging for scraps. It is a matter for congratulation that the plot, from beginning to end, has been thus successfully unearthed, and it is felt on all sides that great credit is due to Inspector Gunning and his skilled coadjutors for the vigilance and promptitude they have displayed throughout the affair."

Loveday read aloud this report, with her feet on the fender of the Lynch Court office.

"Accurate, as far as it goes," she said, as she laid down the paper.

"But we want to know a little more," said Mr. Dyer. "In the first place, I would like to know what it was that diverted your suspicions from the unfortunate Sisters?"

"The way in which they handled the children," answered Loveday promptly. "I have seen female criminals of all kinds handling children, and I have noticed that although they may occasionally—even this is rare—treat them with a certain rough sort of kindness, of tenderness they are utterly incapable. Now Sister Monica, I must admit, is not pleasant to look at; at the same time, there was something absolutely beautiful in the way in which she lifted the little cripple out of the cart, put his tiny thin hand round her neck, and carried him into the house. By-the-way I would like to ask some rapid physiognolmist how he would account for Sister Monica's repulsiveness of feature as contrasted with young Lee's undoubted good looks—heredity, in this case, throws no light on the matter."

"Another question," said Mr. Dyer, not paying much heed to Loveday's digression: "how was it you transferred your suspicions to John Murray?"

"I did not do so immediately, although at the very first it had struck me as odd that he should be so anxious to do the work of the police for them. The chief thing I noticed concerning Murray, on the first and only occasion on which I saw him, was that he had had an accident with his bicycle, for in the right-hand corner of his lamp-glass there was a tiny star, and the lamp itself had a dent on the same side, had also lost its hook, and was fastened to the machine by a bit of electric fuse. The next morning as I was walking up the hill towards Northfield, I was accosted by a young man mounted on that self-same bicycle—not a doubt of it—star in glass, dent, fuse, all three."

"Ah, that sounded an important keynote, and led you to connect Murray and the younger Lee immediately."

"It did, and, of course, also at once gave the lie to his statement that he was a stranger in the place, and confirmed my opinion that there was nothing of the north-countryman in his accent. Other details in his manner and appearance gave rise to other suspicions. For instance, he called himself a press reporter by profession, and his hands were coarse and grimy as only a mechanic's could be. He said he was a bit of a literary man, but the Tennyson that showed so obtrusively from his pocket was new, and in parts uncut, and totally unlike the well-thumbed volume of the literary student. Finally, when he tried and failed to put my latch-key into his waistcoat pocket, I saw the reason lay in the fact that the pocket was already occupied by a soft coil of electric fuse, the end of which protruded. Now, an electric fuse is what an electrical engineer might almost unconsciously carry about with him, it is so essential a part of his working tools, but it is a thing that a literary man or a press reporter could have no possible use for."

"Exactly, exactly. And it was no doubt, that bit of electric fuse that turned your thoughts to the one house in the neighbourhood lighted

CATHERINE LOUISA PIRKIS

by electricity, and suggested to your mind the possibility of electrical engineers turning their talents to account in that direction. Now, will you tell me, what, at that stage of your day's work, induced you to wire to Gunning that you would bring your invisible-ink bottle into use?"

"That was simply a matter or precaution; it did not compel me to the use of invisible ink, if I saw other safe methods of communication. I felt myself being hemmed in on all sides with spies, and I could not tell what emergency might arise. I don't think I have ever had a more difficult game to play. As I walked and talked with the young fellow up the hill, it became clear to me that if I wished to do my work I must lull the suspicions of the gang, and seem to walk into their trap. I saw by the persistent way in which Wootton Hall was forced on my notice that it was wished to fix my suspicions there. I accordingly, to all appearance, did so, and allowed the fellows to think they were making a fool of me."

"Ha! ha! Capital that—the biter bit, with a vengeance! Splendid idea to make that young rascal himself deliver the letter that was to land him and his pals in jail. And he all the time laughing in his sleeve and thinking what a fool he was making of you! Ha, ha, ha!" And Mr. Dyer made the office ring again with his merriment.

"The only person one is at all sorry for in this affair is poor little Sister Anna," said Loveday pityingly; "and yet, perhaps, all things considered, after her sorry experience of life, she may not be so badly placed in a Sisterhood where practical Christianity—not religious hysterics—is the one and only rule of the order."

A Princess's Vengeance

"The girl is young, pretty, friendless and a foreigner, you say, and has disappeared as completely as if the earth had opened to receive her," said Miss Brooke, making a résumé of the facts that Mr. Dyer had been relating to her. "Now, will you tell me why two days were allowed to elapse before the police were communicated with?"

"Mrs. Druce, the lady to whom Lucie Cunier acted as amanuensis," answered Mr. Dyer, "took the matter very calmly at first and said she felt sure that the girl would write to her in a day or so, explaining her extraordinary conduct. Major Druce, her son, the gentleman who came to me this morning, was away from home, on a visit, when the girl took flight. Immediately on his return, however, he communicated the fullest particulars to the police."

"They do not seem to have taken up the case very heartily at Scotland Yard."

"No, they have as good as dropped it. They advised Major Druce to place the matter in my hands, saying that they considered it a case for private rather than police investigation."

"I wonder what made them come to that conclusion."

"I think I can tell you, although the Major seemed quite at a loss on the matter. It seems he had a photograph of the missing girl, which he kept in a drawer of his writing-table. (By-the-way, I think the young man is a good deal 'gone' on this Mdlle. Cunier, in spite of his engagement to another lady.) Well, this portrait he naturally thought would be most useful in helping to trace the girl, and he went to his drawer for it, intending to take it with him to Scotland Yard. To his astonishment, however, it was nowhere to be seen, and, although he at once instituted a rigorous search, and questioned his mother and the servants, one and all, on the matter, it was all to no purpose."

Loveday thought for a moment.

"Well, of course," she said presently "that photograph must have been stolen by someone in the house, and, equally of course, that someone must know more on the matter than he or she cares to avow, and, most probably, has some interest in throwing obstacles in the way of tracing the girl. At the same time, however, the fact in no way disproves the possibility that a crime, and a very black one, may underlie the girl's disappearance."

CATHERINE LOUISA PIRKIS

"The Major himself appears confident that a crime of some sort has been committed, and he grew very excited and a little mixed in his statements more than once just now."

"What sort of woman is the Major's mother?"

"Mrs. Druce? She is rather a well-known personage in certain sets. Her husband died about ten years ago, and since his death she has posed as promoter and propagandist of all sorts of benevolent, though occasionally somewhat visionary ideas; theatrical missions, magic-lantern and playing cards missions, societies for providing perpetual music for the sick poor, for supplying cabmen with comforters, and a hundred other similar schemes have in turn occupied her attention. Her house is a rendezvous for faddists of every description. The latest fad, however, seems to have put all others to flight; it is a scheme for alleviating the condition of 'our sisters in the East,' so she puts it in her prospectus; in other words a Harem Mission on somewhat similar, but I suppose broader lines than the old-fashioned Zenana Mission. This Harem Mission has gathered about her a number of Turkish and Egyptian potentates resident in or visiting London, and has thus incidentally brought about the engagement of her son, Major Druce, with the Princess Dullah-Veih. This Princess is a beauty and an heiress, and although of Turkish parentage, has been brought up under European influence in Cairo."

"Is anything known of the antecedents of Mdlle. Cunier?"

"Very little. She came to Mrs. Druce from a certain Lady Gwynne, who had brought her to England from an orphanage for the daughters of jewellers and watchmakers at Echallets, in Geneva. Lady Gwynne intended to make her governess to her young children, but when she saw that the girl's good looks had attracted her husband's attention, she thought better of it, and suggested to Mrs. Druce that Mademoiselle might be useful to her in conducting her foreign correspondence. Mrs. Druce accordingly engaged the young lady to act as her secretary and amanuensis, and appears, on the whole, to have taken to the girl, and to have been on a pleasant, friendly footing with her. I wonder if the Princess Dullah-Veih was on an equally pleasant footing with her when she saw, as no doubt she did, the attention she received at the Major's hands." (Mr. Dyer shrugged his shoulders.) "The Major's suspicions do not point in that direction, in spite of the fact which I elicited from him by judicious questioning, that the Princess has a violent and jealous temper, and has at times made his life a burden to him. His suspicions centre solely upon a certain Hafiz

Cassimi, son of the Turkish-Egyptian banker of that name. It was at the house of these Cassimis that the Major first met the Princess, and he states that she and young Cassimi are like brother and sister to each other. He says that this young man has had the run of his mother's house and made himself very much at home in it for the past three weeks, ever since, in fact, the Princess came to stay with Mrs. Druce, in order to be initiated into the mysteries of English family life. Hafiz Cassimi, according to the Major's account, fell desperately in love with the little Swiss girl almost at first sight and pestered her with his attentions, and off and on there appear to have passed hot words between the two young men."

"One could scarcely expect a princess with Eastern blood in her veins to be a quiet and passive spectator to such a drama of cross-purposes."

"Scarcely. The Major, perhaps, hardly takes the Princess sufficiently into his reckoning. According to him, young Cassimi is a thorough-going Iago, and he begs me to concentrate attention entirely on him. Cassimi, he says, has stolen the photograph. Cassimi has inveigled the girl out of the house on some pretext—perhaps out of the country also, and he suggests that it might be as well to communicate with the police at Cairo, with as little delay as possible."

"And it hasn't so much as entered his mind that his Princess might have a hand in such a plot as that!"

"Apparently not. I think I told you that Mademoiselle had taken no luggage—not so much as a hand-bag—with her. Nothing, beyond her coat and hat, has disappeared from her wardrobe. Her writing-desk, and, in fact, all her boxes and drawers, have been opened and searched, but no letters or papers of any sort have been found that throw any light upon her movements."

"At what hour in the day is the girl supposed to have left the house?"

"No one can say for certain. It is conjectured that it was some time in the afternoon of the second of this month—a week ago to-day. It was one of Mrs. Druce's big reception days, and with a stream of people going and coming, a young lady, more or less, leaving the house would scarcely be noticed."

"I suppose," said Loveday, after a moment's pause, "this Princess Dullah-Veih has something of a history. One does not often get a Turkish princess in London."

"Yes, she has a history. She is only remotely connected with the present reigning dynasty in Turkey, and I dare say her princess-ship has been made the most of. All the same, however, she has had an altogether exceptional career for an Oriental lady. She was left an orphan at an early age, and was consigned to the guardianship of the elder Cassimi by her relatives. The Cassimis, both father and son, seem to be very advanced and European in their ideas, and by them she was taken to Cairo for her education. About a year ago they 'brought her out' in London, where she made the acquaintance of Major Druce. The young man, by-the-way, appears to be rather hot-headed in his love-making, for within six weeks of his introduction to her their engagement was announced. No doubt it had Mrs. Druce's fullest approval, for knowing her son's extravagant habits and his numerous debts, it must have been patent to her that a rich wife was a necessity to him. The marriage, I believe, was to have taken place this season; but taking into consideration the young man's ill-advised attentions to the little Swiss girl, and the fervour he is throwing into the search for her, I should say it was exceedingly doubtful whether—"

"Major Druce, sir, wishes to see you," said a clerk at that moment, opening the door leading from the outer office.

"Very good; show him in," said Mr. Dyer. Then he turned to Loveday.

"Of course I have spoken to him about you, and he is very anxious to take you to his mother's reception this afternoon, so that you may have a look round and—"

He broke off, having to rise and greet Major Druce, who at that moment entered the room.

He was a tall, handsome young fellow of about seven or eight and twenty, "well turned out" from head to foot, moustache waxed, orchid in button-hole, light kid gloves, and patent leather boots. There was assuredly nothing in his appearance to substantiate his statement to Mr. Dyer that he "hadn't slept a wink all night, that in fact another twenty-four hours of this terrible suspense would send him into his grave."

Mr. Dyer introduced Miss Brooke, and she expressed her sympathy with him on the painful matter that was filling his thoughts.

"It is very good of you, I'm sure," he replied, in a slow, soft drawl, not unpleasant to listen to. "My mother receives this afternoon from half past four to half past six, and I shall be very glad if you will allow me to introduce you to the inside of our house, and to the very ill-looking set that we have somehow managed to gather about us."

"The ill-looking set?"

"Yes; Jews, Turks, heretics and infidels—all there. And they're on the increase too, that's the worst of it. Every week a fresh importation from Cairo."

"Ah, Mrs. Druce is a large-hearted, benevolent woman," interposed Mr. Dyer; "all nationalities gather within her walls."

"Was your mother a large-hearted, benevolent woman?" said the young man, turning upon him. "No! well then, thank Providence that she wasn't; and admit that you know nothing at all on the matter. Miss Brooke," he continued, turning to Loveday, "I've brought round my hansom for you; it's nearly half past four now, and it's a good twenty minutes' drive from here to Portland Place. If you're ready, I'm at your service."

Major Druce's hansom was, like himself, in all respects "well turned out," and the India rubber tires round its wheels allowed an easy flow of conversation to be kept up during the twenty minutes' drive from Lynch Court to Portland Place.

The Major led off the talk in frank and easy fashion.

"My mother," he said, "prides herself on being cosmopolitan in her tastes, and just now we are very cosmopolitan indeed. Even our servants represent divers nationalities; the butler is French, the two footmen Italians, the maids, I believe, are some of them German, some Irish; and I've no doubt if you penetrated to the kitchen-quarters, you'd find the staff there composed in part of Scandinavians, in part of South Sea Islanders. The other quarters of the globe you will find fully represented in the drawing-room."

Loveday had a direct question to ask.

"Are you certain that Mdlle. Cunier had no friends in England?" she said.

"Positive. She hadn't a friend in the world outside my mother's four walls, poor child! She told me more than once that she was 'seule sur la terre.'" He broke off for a moment, as if overcome by a sad memory, then added: "But I'll put a bullet into him, take my word for it, if she isn't found within another twenty-four hours. Personally I should prefer settling the brute in that fashion to handing him over to the police."

His face flushed a deep red, there came a sudden flash to his eye, but for all that, his voice was as soft and slow and unemotional, as though he were talking of nothing more serious than bringing down a partridge.

There fell a brief pause; then Loveday asked another question.

"Is Mademoiselle Catholic or Protestant, can you tell me?"

The Major thought for a moment, then replied:

"'Pon my word, I don't know. She used sometimes to attend a little charge in South Savile Street—I've walked with her occasionally to the church door—but I couldn't for the life of me say whether it was a Catholic, Protestant, or Pagan place of worship. But—but you don't think those confounded priests have—"

"Here, we are in Portland place," interrupted Loveday. "Mrs. Druce's rooms are already full, to judge from that long line of carriages!"

"Miss Brooke," said the Major suddenly, bethinking himself of his responsibilities, "how am I to introduce you? what rôle will you take up this afternoon? Pose as a faddist of some sort, if you want to win my mother's heart. What do you say to having started a grand scheme for supplying Hottentots and Kaffirs with eye-glasses? My mother would swear eternal friendship with you at once."

"Don't introduce me at all at first," answered Loveday. "Get me into some quiet corner, where I can see without being seen. Later on in the afternoon, when I have had time to look round a little, I'll tell you whether it will be necessary to introduce me or not."

"It will be a mob this afternoon, and no mistake," said Major Druce, as side by side, they entered the house. "Do you hear that fizzing and clucking just behind us? That's Arabic; you'll get it in whiffs between gusts of French and German all the afternoon. The Egyptian contingent seems to be in full force to-day. I don't see any Choctaw Indians, but no doubt they'll send their representatives later on. Come in at this side door, and we'll work our way round to that big palm. My mother is sure to be at the principal doorway."

The drawing rooms were packed from end to end, and Major Druce's progress, as he headed Loveday through the crowd, was impeded by hand-shaking and the interchange of civilities with his mother's guests.

Eventually the big palm standing in a Chinese cistern was reached, and there, half screened from view by its graceful branches, he placed a chair for Miss Brooke.

From this quiet nook, as now and again the crowd parted, Loveday could command a fair view of both drawing-rooms.

"Don't attract attention to me by standing at my elbow," she whispered to the Major.

He answered her whisper with another.

"There's the Beast—Iago, I mean," he said; "do you see him? He's standing talking to that fair, handsome woman in pale green, with a picture hat. She's Lady Gwynne. And there's my mother, and there's Dolly—the Princess I mean—alone on the sofa. Ah! you can't see her now for the crowd. Yes, I'll go, but if you want me, just nod to me and I shall understand."

If was easy to see what had brought such a fashionable crowd to Mrs. Druce's rooms that afternoon. Every caller, as soon as she had shaken hands with the hostess, passed on to the Princess's sofa, and there waited patiently till opportunity presented itself for an introduction to her Eastern Highness.

Loveday found it impossible to get more than the merest glimpse of her, and so transferred her attention to Mr. Hafiz Cassimi, who had been referred to in such unceremonious language by Major Druce.

He was a swarthy, well-featured man, with bold, black eyes, and lips that had the habit of parting now and again, not to smile, but as if for no other purpose than to show a double row of gleaming white teeth. The European dress he wore seemed to accord ill with the man; and Loveday could fancy that those black eyes and that double row of white teeth would have shown to better advantage beneath a turban or a fez cap. From Cassimi, her eye wandered to Mrs. Druce—a tall, stout woman, dressed in black velvet, and with hair mounted high on her head, that had the appearance of being either bleached or powdered. She gave Loveday the impression of being that essentially modern product of modern society—the woman who combines in one person the hard-working philanthropist with the hard-working woman of fashion. As arrivals began to slacken, she left her post near the door and began to make the round of the room. From snatches of talk that came to her where she sat, Loveday could gather that with one hand, as it were, this energetic lady was organizing a grand charity concert, and with the other pushing the interests of a big ball that was shortly to be given by the officers of her son's regiment.

It was a hot June day. In spite of closed blinds and open windows, the rooms were stifling to a degree. The butler, a small dark, slight Frenchman, made his way through the throng to a window at Loveday's right hand, to see if a little more air could be admitted.

Major Druce followed on his heels to Loveday's side.

"Will you come into the next room and have some tea?" he asked; "I'm sure you must feel nearly suffocated here." He broke off, then added in a lower tone: "I hope you have kept your eyes on the Beast. Did you ever in your life see a more repulsive-looking animal?"

Loveday took his questions in their order.

"No tea, thank you," she said, "but I shall be glad if you will tell your butler to bring me a glass of water—there he is, at your elbow. Yes, off and on I have been studying Mr. Cassimi, and I must admit I do not like his smileless smile."

The butler brought the water. The Major, much to his annoyance, was seized upon simultaneously by two ladies, one eager to know if any tidings had been received of Mdlle. Cunier, the other anxious to learn if a distinguished president to the Harem Mission had been decided upon.

Soon after six the rooms began to thin somewhat, and presentations to the Princess ceasing, Loveday was able to get a full view of her.

She presented a striking picture, seated, half-reclining, on a sofa, with two white-robed, dark-skinned Egyptian maidens standing behind it. A more unfortunate sobriquet than "Dolly" could scarcely have been found by the Major for this Oriental beauty, with her olive complexion, her flashing eyes and extravagant richness of attire.

"'Queen of Sheba' would be far more appropriate," thought Loveday. "She turns the commonplace sofa into a throne, and, I should say, makes every one of those ladies feel as if she ought to have donned court dress and plumes for the occasion."

It was difficult for her, from where she sat, to follow the details of the Princess's dress. She could only see that a quantity of soft orange-tinted silk was wound about the upper part of her arms and fell from her shoulders like drooping wings, and that here and there jewels flashed out from its folds. Her thick black hair was loosely knotted, and kept in its place by jeweled pins and a bandeau of pearls; and similar bandeaus adored her slender throat and wrists.

"Are you lost in admiration?" said the Major, once more at her elbow, in a slightly sarcastic tone. "That sort of thing is very taking and effective at first, but after a time—"

He did not finish his sentence, shrugged his shoulders and walked away. Half-past six chimed from a small clock on a bracket. Carriage after carriage was rolling away from the door now, and progress on the stairs was rendered difficult by a descending crowd.

A quarter to seven struck, the last hand-shaking had been gone through, and Mrs. Druce, looking hot and tired, had sunk into a chair at the Princess's right hand, bending slightly forward to render conversation with her easy.

On the Princess's left hand, Lady Gwynne had taken a chair, and sat in converse with Hafiz Cassimi, who stood beside her.

Evidently these four were on very easy and intimate terms with each other. Lady Gwynne had tossed her big picture hat on a chair at her left hand, and was fanning herself with a palm-leaf. Mrs. Druce, beckoning to the butler, desired him to bring them some claret-cup from the refreshment-room.

No one seemed to observe Loveday seated still in her nook beside the big palm.

She signaled to the Major, who stood looking discontentedly from one of the windows.

"That is a most interesting group," she said; "now, if you like, you may introduce me to your mother."

"Oh, with pleasure—under what name?" he asked.

"Under my own," she answered, "and please be very distinct in pronouncing it, raise your voice slightly so that every one of those persons may hear it. And then, please add my profession, and say I am here at your request to investigate the circumstances connected with Mdlle. Cunier's disappearance."

Major Druce looked astounded.

"But—but," he stammered, "have you seen anything—found out anything? If not, don't you think it will be better to preserve your incognita a little longer."

"Don't stop to ask questions," said Loveday sharply; "now, this very minute, do what I ask you, or the opportunity will be gone."

The Major without further demur, escorted Loveday across the room. The conversation between the four intimate friends had now become general and animated, and he had to wait for a minute or so before he could get an opportunity to speak to his mother.

During that minute Loveday stood a little in his rear, with Lady Gwynne and Cassimi at her right hand.

"I want to introduce this lady to you," said the Major, when a pause in the talk gave him his opportunity. "This is Miss Loveday Brooke, a lady detective, and she is here at my request to investigate the circumstances connected with the disappearance of Mdlle. Cunier."

He said the words slowly and distinctly.

"There!" he said to himself complacently, as he ended; "if I had been reading the lessons in church, I couldn't have been more emphatic."

A blank silence for a moment fell upon the group, and even the butler, just then entering with the claret-cup, came to a standstill at the door.

Then, simultaneously, a glance flashed from Mrs. Druce to Lady Gwynne, from Lady Gwynne to Mrs. Druce, and then, also simultaneously, the eyes of both ladies rested, though only for an instant, on the big picture hat lying on the chair.

Lady Gwynne started to her feet and seized her hat, adjusting it without so much as a glance at a mirror.

"I must go at once; this very minute," she said. "I promised Charlie I would back soon after six, and now it is past seven. Mr. Cassimi, will you take me down to my carriage?" And with the most hurried of leave-takings to the Princess and her hostess, the lady swept out of the room, followed by Mr. Cassimi.

The butler still standing at the door, drew back to allow the lady to pass, and then, claret-cup and all, followed her out of the room.

Mrs. Druce drew a long breath and bowed formally to Loveday.

"I was a little taken by surprise," she began—

But here the Princess rose suddenly from the sofa.

"Moi, je suis fatiguée," she said in excellent French to Mrs. Druce, and she too swept out of the room, throwing, as she passed, what seemed to Loveday a slightly scornful glance towards the Major.

Her two attendants, one carrying her fan, and the other her reclining cushions, followed.

Mrs. Druce again turned to Loveday.

"Yes, I confess I was taken a little by surprise," she said, her manner thawing slightly. "I am not accustomed to the presence of detectives in my house; but now tell me what do you propose doing: how do you mean to begin your investigations—by going over the house and looking in all the corners, or by cross-questioning the servants? Forgive my asking, but really I am quite at a loss; I haven't the remotest idea how such investigations are generally conducted."

"I do not propose to do much in the way of investigation to-night," answered Loveday as formally as she had been addressed, "for I have very important business to transact before eight o'clock this evening. I shall ask you to allow me to see Mdlle. Cunier's room—ten minutes there will be sufficient—after that, I do not think I need further trouble you."

"Certainly; by all means," answered Mrs. Druce; "you'll find the room exactly as Lucie left it, nothing has been disturbed."

She turned to the butler, who had by this time returned and stood presenting the claret-cup, and, in French, desired him to summon her maid, and tell her to show Miss Brooke to Mdlle. Cunier's room.

The ten minutes that Loveday had said would suffice for her survey of this room extended themselves to fifteen, but the extra five minutes assuredly were not expended by her in the investigation of drawers and boxes. The maid, a pleasant, well-spoken young woman, jingled her keys, and opened every lock, and seemed not at all disinclined to enter into the light gossip that Loveday contrived to set going.

She answered freely a variety of questions that Loveday put to her respecting Mademoiselle and her general habits, and from Mademoiselle, the talk drifted to other members of Mrs. Druce's household.

If Loveday had, as she had stated, important business to transact that evening, she certainly set about it in a strange fashion.

After she quitted Mademoiselle's room, she went straight out of the house, without leaving a message of any sort for either Mrs. or Major Druce. She walked the length of Portland Place in leisurely fashion, and then, having first ascertained that her movements were not being watched, she called a hansom, and desired the man to drive her to Madame Celine's, a fashionable milliner's in Old Bond Street.

At Madame Celine's she spent close upon half-an-hour, giving many and minute directions for the making of a hat, which assuredly, when finished, would compare with nothing in the way of millinery that she had ever before put upon her head.

From Madame Celine's the hansom conveyed her to an undertaker's shop, at the corner of South Savile Street, and here she spent a brief ten minutes in conversation with the undertaker himself in his little back parlour.

From the undertaker's she drove home to her rooms in Gower Street, and then, before she divested herself of hat and coat, she wrote a brief note to Major Druce, requesting him to meet her on the following morning at Eglacé's, the confectioner's, in South Savile Street, at nine o'clock punctually.

This note she committed to the charge of the cab-driver, desiring him to deliver it at Portland Place on his way back to his stand.

"They've queer ways of doing things—these people!" said the Major, as he opened and read the note. "Suppose I must keep the appointment though, confound it. I can't see that she can possibly have found out anything by just sitting still in a corner for a couple of hours! And I'm confident she didn't give that beast Cassimi one quarter the attention she bestowed on other people."

In spite of his grumbling, however, the Major kept his appointment, and nine o'clock the next morning saw him shaking hands with Miss Brooke on Eglacé's doorstep.

"Dismiss your hansom," she said to him. "I only want you to come a few doors down the street, to the French Protestant church, to which you have sometimes escorted Mdlle. Cunier."

At the church door Loveday paused a moment.

"Before we enter," she said, "I want you to promise that whatever you may see going on there—however greatly you may be surprised—you will make no disturbance, not so much as open your lips till we come out."

The Major, not a little bewildered, gave the required promise; and, side by side, the two entered the church.

It was little more than a big room; at the farther end, in the middle of the nave, stood the pulpit, and immediately behind this was a low platform, enclosed by a brass rail.

Behind this brass rail, in black Geneva gown, stood the pastor of the church, and before him, on cushions, kneeled two persons, a man and a woman.

These two persons and an old man, the verger, formed the whole of the congregation. The position of the church, amid shops and narrow back-yards, had necessitated the filling in of every one of its windows with stained glass; it was, consequently, so dim that, coming in from the outside glare of sunlight, the Major found it difficult to make out what was going on at the farther end.

The verger came forward and offered to show them to a seat. Loveday shook her head—they would be leaving in a minute, she said, and would prefer standing where they were.

The Major began to take in the situation.

"Why they're being married!" he said in a loud whisper. "What on earth have you brought me in here for?"

Loveday laid her finger on her lips and frowned severely at him.

The marriage service came to an end, the pastor extended his black-gowned arms like the wings of a bat and pronounced the benediction; the man and woman rose from their knees and proceeded to follow him into the vestry.

The woman was neatly dressed in a long dove-coloured travelling cloak. She wore a large hat, from which fell a white gossamer veil that completely hid her face from view. The man was small, dark and slight, and as he passed on to the vestry beside his bride, the Major at once identified him as his mother's butler.

"Why, that's Lebrun!" he said in a still louder whisper than before. "Why, in the name of all that's wonderful, have you brought me here to see that fellow married?"

"You'd better come outside if you can't keep quiet," said Loveday severely, and leading the way out of the church as she spoke.

Outside, South Savile Street was busy with early morning traffic.

"Let us go back to Eglacé's" said Loveday, "and have some coffee. I will explain to you there all you are wishing to know."

But before the coffee could be brought to them, the Major had asked at least a dozen questions.

Loveday put them all on one side.

"All in good time" she said. "You are leaving out the most important question of all. Have you no curiosity to know who was the bride that Lebrun has chosen?"

"I don't suppose it concerns me in the slightest degree," he answered indifferently; "but since you wish me to ask the question—Who was she?"

"Lucie Cunier, lately your mother's amanuensis."

"The—!" cried the Major, jumping to his feet and uttering an exclamation that must be indicated by a blank.

"Take it calmly," said Loveday; "don't rave. Sit down and I'll tell you all about it. No, it is not the doing of your friend Cassimi, so you need not threaten to put a bullet into him; the girl has married Lebrun of her own free will—no one has forced her into it."

"Lucie has married Lebrun of her own free will!" he echoed, growing very white and taking the chair which faced Loveday at the little table.

"Will you have sugar?" asked Loveday, stirring the coffee, which the waiter at that moment brought.

"Yes, I repeat," she presently resumed, "Lucie has married Lebrun of her own free will, although I conjecture she might not perhaps have been quite so willing to crown his happiness if the Princess Dullah-Veih had not made it greatly to her interest to do so."

"Dolly made it to her interest to do so?" again echoed the Major.

"Do not interrupt me with exclamations; let me tell the story my own fashion, and then you may ask as many questions as you please. Now, to begin at the beginning, Lucie became engaged to Lebrun within a month of her coming to your mother's house, but she carefully kept the secret from everyone, even from the servants, until about a month ago, when she mentioned the fact in confidence to Mrs. Druce in order to defend herself from the charge of having sought to attract your attention. There was nothing surprising in this engagement; they were both lonely and in a foreign land, spoke the same language, and no doubt had many things in common; and, although chance has lifted Lucie somewhat out of her station, she really belongs to the same class in life as Lebrun. Their love-making appears to have run along smoothly enough until you came home on leave, and the girl's pretty face attracted your attention. Your evident admiration for her disturbed the equanimity of the Princess, who saw your devotion to herself waning; of Lebrun, who fancied Lucie's manner to him had changed; of your mother, who was anxious that you should make a suitable marriage. Also additional complications arose from the fact that your attentions to the little Swiss girl had drawn Mr. Cassimi's notice to her numerous attractions, and there was the danger of you two young men posing as rivals. At this juncture Lady Gwynne, as an intimate friend, and one who had herself suffered a twinge of heartache on Mademoiselle's account, was taken into your mother's confidence, and the three ladies in council decided that Lucie, in some fashion, must be got out of the way before you, and Mr. Cassimi came to an open breach, or you had spoilt your matrimonial prospects."

Here the Major made a slightly impatient movement.

Loveday went on: "It was the Princess who solved the question how this was to be done. Fair Rosamonds are no longer put out of the way by 'a cup of cold poison'—golden guineas do the thing far more easily and innocently. The Princess expressed her willingness to bestow a thousand pounds on Lucie on the day that she married Lebrun, and to set her up afterwards as a fashionable milliner in Paris. After this munificent offer, everything else became mere matter of detail. The main thing was to get the damsel out of the way without your being able to trace her—perhaps work on her feelings, and induce her, at the last moment, to throw over Lebrun. Your absence from home, on a three days' visit, gave them the wished-for opportunity. Lady Gwynne took her milliner into her confidence. Madame Celine consented to receive Lucie into her house, seclude her in a room on the upper floor, and at the same time give her an insight into the profession of a fashionable milliner. The rest I think you know. Lucie quietly walks out of the house one afternoon, taking no luggage, calling no cab, and thereby cutting off one very obvious means of being traced. Madame Celine receives and hides her—not a difficult feat to accomplish in London, more especially if the one to be hidden is a foreign amanuensis, who is seldom seen out of doors, and who leaves no photograph behind her."

"I suppose it was Lebrun who had the confounded cheek to go to my drawer and appropriate that photograph. I wish it had been Cassimi—I could have kicked him, but—but it makes one feel rather small to have posed as rival to one's mother's butler."

"I think you may congratulate yourself that Lebrun did nothing worse than go to your drawer and appropriate that photograph. I never saw a man bestow a more deadly look of hatred than he threw at you yesterday afternoon in your mother's drawing-room; it was that look of hatred that first drew my attention to the man and set me on the track that has ended in the Swiss Protestant church this morning."

"Ah! let me hear about that—let me have the links in the chain, one by one, as you came upon them," said the Major.

He was still pale—almost as the marble table at which they sat, but his voice had gone back to its normal slow, soft drawl.

"With pleasure. The look that Lebrun threw at you, as he crossed the room to open the window, was link number one. As I saw that look, I said to myself there is someone in that corner whom that man hates with a deadly hatred. Then you came forward to speak to me, and I saw that it was you that the man was ready to murder, if opportunity offered. After this, I scrutinized him closely—not a detail of his features or his dress escaped me, and I noticed, among other things, that on the fourth finger of his left hand, half hidden by a more pretentious ring, was an old fashioned curious looking silver one. That silver ring was link number two in the chain."

"Ah, I suppose you asked for that glass of water on purpose to get a closer view of the ring?"

"I did, I found it was a Genevese ring of ancient make, the like of which I had not seen since I was a child and played with one, that my old Swiss bonne used to wear. Now I must tell you a little bit of Genevese history before I can make you understand how important a link that silver ring was to me. Echallets, the town in which Lucie was born, and her father had kept a watchmaker's shop, has long been famous for its jewellery and watchmaking. The two trades, however, were not combined in one until about a hundred years ago, when the corporation of the town passed a law decreeing that they should unite in one guild for their common good. To celebrate this amalgamation of interests, the jewellers fabricated a certain number of silver rings, consisting of a plain band of silver, on which two hands, in relief, clasped each other. These rings were distributed among the members of the guild, and as time has gone on they have become scarce and valuable as relics of the past. In certain families, they have been handed down as heirlooms, and have frequently done duty as betrothal rings—the clasped hands no doubt suggesting their suitability for this purpose. Now, when I saw such a ring on Lebrun's finger, I naturally guessed from whom he had received it, and at once classed his interests with those of your mother and the Princess, and looked upon him as their possible coadjutor."

"What made you throw the brute Cassimi altogether out of your reckoning?"

"I did not do so at this stage of events; only, so to speak, marked him as 'doubtful' and kept my eye on him. I determined to try an experiment that I have never before attempted in my work. You know what that experiment was. I saw five persons, Mrs. Druce, the Princess, Lady Gwynne, Mr. Cassimi and Lebrun all in the room within a few yards of each other, and I asked you to take them by surprise and announce my name and profession, so that every one of those five persons could hear you."

"You did. I could not, for the life of me, make out what was your motive for so doing."

"My motive for so doing was simply, as it were, to raise the sudden cry, 'The enemy is upon you,' and to set every one of those five persons guarding their weak point—that is, if they had one. I'll draw your attention to what followed. Mr. Cassimi remained nonchalant and impassive; your mother and Lady Gwynne exchanged glances, and they both simultaneously threw a nervous look at Lady Gwynne's hat lying on the chair. Now as I had stood waiting to be introduced to Mrs. Druce, I had casually read the name of Madame Céline on the lining of the hat and I at once concluded that Madame Céline must be a very weak point indeed; a conclusion that was confirmed when Lady Gwynne hurriedly seized her hat and as hurriedly departed. Then the Princess scarcely less abruptly rose and left the room, and Lebrun on the point of entering, quitted it also. When he returned five minutes later, with the claret-cup, he had removed the ring from his finger, so I had now little doubt where his weak point lay."

"It's wonderful; it's like a fairy tale!," drawled the Major. "Pray, go on."

"After this," continued Loveday, "my work became very simple. I did not care two straws for seeing Mademoiselle's room, but I cared very much to have a talk with Mrs. Druce's maid. From her I elicited the important fact that Lebrun was leaving very unexpectedly on the following day, and that his boxes were packed and labeled for Paris. After I left your house, I drove to Madame Céline's, and there, as a sort of entrance fee, ordered an elaborate hat. I praised freely the hats they had on view, and while giving minute directions as to the one I required, I extracted the information that Madame Céline had recently taken on a new milliner who had very great artistic skill. Upon this, I asked permission to see this new milliner and give her special instructions concerning my hat. My request was referred to Madame Céline, who appeared much ruffled by it, and informed me that it would be quite useless for me to see this new milliner; she could execute no more orders, as she was leaving the next day for Paris, where she intended opening an establishment on her own account.

"Now you see the point at which I had arrived. There was Lebrun and there was this new milliner each leaving for Paris on the same day; it was not unreasonable to suppose that they might start in company, and that before so doing, a little ceremony might be gone through in the Swiss Protestant church that Mademoiselle occasionally attended. This conjecture sent me to the undertaker in South Savile Street, who combines with his undertaking the office of verger to the little church. From him I learned that a marriage was to take place at the church at a quarter to nine the next morning and that the names of the contracting parties were Pierre Lebrun and Lucie Cuénin."

"Cuénin!"

"Yes, that is the girl's real name; it seems Lady Gwynne re-christened her Cunier, because she said the English pronunciation of Cuénin grated on her ear—people would insist upon adding a *g* after the *n*. She introduced her to Mrs. Druce under the name of Cunier, forgetting, perhaps, the girl's real name, or else thinking it a matter of no importance. This fact, no doubt, considerably lessened Lebrun's fear of detection in procuring his licence and transmitting it to the Swiss pastor. Perhaps you are a little surprised at my knowledge of the facts I related to you at the beginning of our conversation. I got at them through Lebrun this morning. At half-past eight I went down to the church and found him there, waiting for his bride. He grew terribly excited at seeing me, and thought I was going to bring you down on him and upset his wedding arrangements at the last moment. I assured him to the contrary, and his version of the facts I have handed on to you. Should, however, any details of the story seem to you to be lacking, I have no doubt that Mrs. Druce or the Princess will supply them, now that all necessity for secrecy has come to an end."

The Major drew on his gloves; his colour had come back to him; he had resumed his easy suavity of manner.

"I don't think," he said slowly, "I'll trouble my mother or the Princess; and I shall be glad, if you have the opportunity, if you will make people understand that I only moved in the matter at all out of—of mere kindness to a young and friendless foreigner."

Drawn Daggers

I admit that the dagger business is something of a puzzle to me, but as for the lost necklace—well, I should have thought a child would have understood that," said Mr. Dyer irritably. "When a young lady loses a valuable article of jewellery and wishes to hush the matter up, the explanation is obvious."

"Sometimes," answered Miss Brooke calmly, "the explanation that is obvious is the one to be rejected, not accepted."

Off and on these two had been, so to speak, "jangling" a good deal that morning. Perhaps the fact was in part to be attributed to the biting east wind which had set Loveday's eyes watering with the gritty dust, as she had made her way to Lynch Court, and which was, at the present moment, sending the smoke, in aggravating gusts, down the chimney into Mr. Dyer's face. Thus it was, however. On the various topics that had chanced to come up for discussion that morning between Mr. Dyer and his colleague, they had each taken up, as if by design, diametrically opposite points of view.

His temper altogether gave way now.

"If," he said, bringing his hand down with emphasis on his writing table, "you lay it down as a principle that the obvious is to be rejected in favour of the abstruse, you'll soon find yourself launched in the predicament of having to prove that two apples added to two other apples do not make four. But there, if you don't choose to see things from my point of view, that is no reason why you should lose your temper!"

"Mr. Hawke wishes to see you, sir," said a clerk, at that moment entering the room.

It was a fortunate diversion. Whatever might be the differences of opinion in which these two might indulge in private, they were careful never to parade those differences before their clients.

Mr. Dyer's irritability vanished in a moment.

"Show the gentleman in," he said to the clerk. Then he turned to Loveday. "This is the Rev. Anthony Hawke, the gentleman at whose house I told you that Miss Monroe is staying temporarily. He is a clergyman of the Church of England, but gave up his living some twenty years ago when he married a wealthy lady. Miss Monroe has been sent over to his guardianship from Pekin by her father, Sir George

CATHERINE LOUISA PIRKIS

Monroe, in order to get her out of the way of a troublesome and undesirable suitor."

The last sentence was added in a low and hurried tone, for Mr. Hawke was at that moment entering the room.

He was a man close upon sixty years of age, white-haired, clean shaven, with a full, round face, to which a small nose imparted a somewhat infantine expression. His manner of greeting was urbane but slightly flurried and nervous. He gave Loveday the impression of being an easy-going, happy-tempered man who, for the moment, was unusually disturbed and perplexed.

He glanced uneasily at Loveday. Mr. Dyer hastened to explain that this was the lady by whose aid he hoped to get to the bottom of the matter now under consideration.

"In that case there can be no objection to my showing you this," said Mr. Hawke; "it came by post this morning. You see my enemy still pursues me."

As he spoke he took from his pocket a big, square envelope, from which he drew a large-sized sheet of paper.

On this sheet of paper were roughly drawn, in ink, two daggers, about six inches in length, with remarkably pointed blades.

Mr. Dyer looked at the sketch with interest.

"We will compare this drawing and its envelope with those you previously received," he said, opening a drawer of his writing-table and taking thence a precisely similar envelope. On the sheet of paper, however, that this envelope enclosed, there was drawn one dagger only.

He placed both envelopes and their enclosures side by side, and in silence compared them. Then, without a word, he handed them to Miss Brooke, who, taking a glass from her pocket, subjected them to a similar careful and minute scrutiny.

Both envelopes were of precisely the same make, and were each addressed to Mr. Hawke's London address in a round, school-boyish, copy-book sort of hand—the hand so easy to write and so difficult to being home to any writer on account of its want of individuality. Each envelope likewise bore a Cork and a London postmark.

The sheet of paper, however, that the first envelope enclosed bore the sketch of one dagger only.

Loveday laid down her glass.

"The envelopes," she said, "have, undoubtedly, been addressed by the same person, but these last two daggers have not been drawn by the hand that drew the first. Dagger number one was, evidently, drawn by a timid, uncertain and inartistic hand—see how the lines wave and how they have been patched here and there. The person who drew the other daggers, I should say, could do better work; the outline, though rugged, is bold and free. I should like to take these sketches home with me and compare them again at my leisure."

"Ah, I felt sure what your opinion would be!" said Mr. Dyer complacently.

Mr. Hawke seemed much disturbed.

"Good gracious!" he exclaimed; "you don't mean to say I have two enemies pursuing me in this fashion! What does it mean? Can it be—is it possible, do you think, that these things have been sent to me by the members of some Secret Society in Ireland—under error, of course—mistaking me for someone else? They can't be meant for me; I have never, in my whole life, been mixed up with any political agitation of any sort."

Mr. Dyer shook his head. "Members of secret societies generally make pretty sure of their ground before they send out missives of this kind," he said. "I have never heard of such an error being made. I think, too, we mustn't build any theories on the Irish post-mark; the letters may have been posted in Cork for the whole and sole purpose of drawing off attention from some other quarter."

"Will you mind telling me a little about the loss of the necklace?" here said Loveday, bringing the conversation suddenly round from the daggers to the diamonds.

"I think," interposed Mr. Dyers, turning towards her, "that the episode of the drawn daggers—drawn in a double sense—should be treated entirely on its own merits, considered as a thing apart from the loss of the necklace. I am inclined to believe that when we have gone a little further into the matter we shall find that each circumstance belongs to a different group of facts. After all, it is possible that these daggers may have been sent by way of a joke—a rather foolish one, I admit—by some harum-scarum fellow bent on causing a sensation."

Mr. Hawke's face brightened.

"Ah! now, do you think so—really think so?" he exclaimed. "It would lift such a load from my mind if you could bring the thing home, in this way, to some practical joker. There are a lot of such fellows knocking about the world. Why, now I come to think of it, my nephew, Jack, who is a good deal with us just now, and is not quite so steady a fellow as I should like him to be, must have a good many such scamps among his acquaintances."

"A good many such scamps among his acquaintances," echoed Loveday; "that certainly gives plausibility to Mr. Dyer's supposition. At the same time, I think we are bound to look at the other side of the case, and admit the possibility of these daggers being sent in right-down sober earnest by persons concerned in the robbery, with the intention of intimidating you and preventing full investigation of the matter. If this be so, it will not signify which thread we take up and follow. If we find the sender of the daggers we are safe to come upon the thief; or, if we follow up and find the thief, the sender of the daggers will not be far off."

Mr. Hawke's face fell once more.

"It's an uncomfortable position to be in," he said slowly. "I suppose, whoever they are, they will do the regulation thing, and next time will send an instalment of three daggers, in which case I may consider myself a doomed man. It did not occur to me before, but I remember now that I did not receive the first dagger until after I had spoken very strongly to Mrs. Hawke, before the servants, about my wish to set the police to work. I told her I felt bound, in honour to Sir George, to do so, as the necklace had been lost under my roof."

"Did Mrs. Hawke object to your calling in the aid of the police?" asked Loveday.

"Yes, most strongly. She entirely supported Miss Monroe in her wish to take no steps in the matter. Indeed, I should not have come round as I did last night to Mr. Dyer, if my wife had not been suddenly summoned from home by the serious illness of her sister. At least," he corrected himself with a little attempt at self-assertion, "my coming to him might have been a little delayed. I hope you understand, Mr. Dyer; I do not mean to imply that I am not master in my own house."

"Oh, quite so, quite so," responded Mr. Dyer. "Did Mrs. Hawke or Miss Monroe give any reasons for not wishing you to move in the matter?"

"All told, I should think they gave about a hundred reasons—I can't remember them all. For one thing, Miss Monroe said it might necessitate her appearing in the police courts, a thing she would not consent to do; and she certainly did not consider the necklace was worth the fuss I was making over it. And that necklace, sir, has been valued at over nine hundred pounds, and has come down to the young lady from her mother."

"And Mrs. Hawke?"

"Mrs. Hawke supported Miss Monroe in her views in her presence. But privately to me afterwards, she gave other reasons for not wishing the police called in. Girls, she said, were always careless with their jewellery, she might have lost the necklace in Pekin, and never have brought it to England at all."

"Quite so," said Mr. Dyer. "I think I understood you to say that no one had seen the necklace since Miss Monroe's arrival in England. Also, I believe it was she who first discovered it to be missing?"

"Yes. Sir George, when he wrote apprising me of his daughter's visit, added a postscript to his letter, saying that his daughter was bringing her necklace with her and that he would feel greatly obliged if I would have it deposited with as little delay as possible at my bankers', where it could be easily got at if required. I spoke to Miss Monroe about doing this two or three times, but she did not seem at all inclined to comply with her father's wishes. Then my wife took the matter in hand— Mrs. Hawke, I must tell you, has a very firm, resolute manner—she told Miss Monroe plainly that she would not have the responsibility of those diamonds in the house, and insisted that there and then they should be sent off to the bankers. Upon this Miss Monroe went up to her room, and presently returned, saying that her necklace had disappeared. She herself, she said, had placed it in her jewel-case and the jewel-case in her wardrobe, when her boxes were unpacked. The jewel-case was in the wardrobe right enough, and no other article of jewellery appeared to have been disturbed, but the little padded niche in which the necklace had been deposited was empty. My wife and her maid went upstairs immediately, and searched every corner of the room, but, I'm sorry to say, without any result."

"Miss Monroe, I suppose, has her own maid?"

"No, she has not. The maid—an elderly native woman—who left Pekin with her, suffered so terribly from sea-sickness that, when they reached Malta, Miss Monroe allowed her to land and remain there in charge of an agent of the P. and O. Company till an outward bound packet could take her back to China. It seems the poor woman thought she was going to die, and was in a terrible state of mind because she hadn't brought her coffin with her. I dare say you know the terror these Chinese have of being buried in foreign soil. After her departure, Miss Monroe engaged one of the steerage passengers to act as her maid for the remainder of the voyage."

"Did Miss Monroe make the long journey from Pekin accompanied only by this native woman?"

"No; friends escorted her to Hong King—by far the roughest part of the journey. From Hong Kong she came on in *The Colombo*, accompanied only by her maid. I wrote and told her father I would meet her at the docks in London; the young lady, however, preferred landing at Plymouth, and telegraphed to me from there that she was coming on by rail to Waterloo, where, if I liked, I might meet her."

"She seems to be a young lady of independent habits. Was she brought up and educated in China?"

"Yes; by a succession of French and American governesses. After her mother's death, when she was little more than a baby, Sir George could not make up his mind to part with her, as she was his only child."

"I suppose you and Sir George Monroe are old friends?"

"Yes; he and I were great chums before he went out to China—now about twenty years ago—and it was only natural, when he wished to get his daughter out of the way of young Danvers's impertinent attentions, that he should ask me to take charge of her till he could claim his retiring pension and set up his tent in England."

"What was the chief objection to Mr. Danvers's attentions?"

"Well, he is only a boy of one-and-twenty, and has no money into the bargain. He has been sent out to Pekin by his father to study the language, in order to qualify for a billet in the customs, and it may be a dozen years before he is in a position to keep a wife. Now, Miss Monroe is an heiress—will come into her mother's large fortune when she is of age—and Sir George, naturally, would like her to make a good match."

"I suppose Miss Monroe came to England very reluctantly?"

"I imagine so. No doubt it was a great wrench for her to leave her home and friends in that sudden fashion and come to us, who are, one and all, utter strangers to her. She is very quiet, very shy and reserved. She goes nowhere, sees no one. When some old China friends of her father's called to see her the other day, she immediately found she had a headache, and went to bed. I think, on the whole, she gets on better with my nephew than with anyone else."

"Will you kindly tell me of how many persons your household consists at the present moment?

"At the present moment we are one more than usual, for my nephew, Jack, is home with his regiment from India, and is staying with us. As a rule, my household consists of my wife and myself, butler, cook, housemaid and my wife's maid, who just now is doing double duty as Miss Monroe's maid also."

Mr. Dyer looked at his watch.

"I have an important engagement in ten minutes' time," he said, "so I must leave you and Miss Brooke to arrange details as to how and when she is to begin her work inside your house, for, of course, in a case of this sort we must, in the first instance at any rate, concentrate attention within your four walls."

"The less delay the better," said Loveday. "I should like to attack the mystery at once—this afternoon."

Mr. Hawke thought for a moment.

"According to present arrangements," he said, with a little hesitation, "Mrs. Hawke will return next Friday, that is the day after to-morrow, so I can only ask you to remain in the house till the morning of that day. I'm sure you will understand that there might be some—some little awkwardness in—"

"Oh, quite so," interrupted Loveday. "I don't see at present that there will be any necessity for me to sleep in the house at all. How would it be for me to assume the part of a lady house decorator in the employment of a West-end firm, and sent by them to survey your house and advise upon its re-decoration? All I should have to do, would be to walk about your rooms with my head on one side, and a pencil and note-book in my hand. I should interfere with no one, your family life would go on as usual, and I could make my work as short or as long as necessity might dictate."

Mr. Hawke had no objection to offer to this. He had, however, a request to make as he rose to depart, and he made it a little nervously.

"If," he said, "by any chance there should come a telegram from Mrs. Hawke, saying she will return by an earlier train, I suppose—I hope, that is, you will make some excuse, and—and not get me into hot water, I mean."

To this, Loveday answered a little evasively that she trusted no such telegram would be forthcoming, but that, in any case, he might rely upon her discretion.

FOUR O'CLOCK WAS STRIKING FROM a neighbouring church clock as Loveday lifted the old-fashioned brass knocker of Mr. Hawke's house in Tavistock Square. An elderly butler admitted her and showed her into the drawing-room on the first floor. A single glance round showed Loveday that if her rôle had been real instead of assumed, she would have found plenty of scope for her talents. Although the house was in all respects comfortably furnished, it bore unmistakably the impress of those early Victorian days when aesthetic surroundings were not deemed a necessity of existence; an impress which people past middle age, and growing increasingly indifferent to the accessories of life, are frequently careless to remove.

"Young life here is evidently an excrescence, not part of the home; a troop of daughters turned into this room would speedily set going a different condition of things," thought Loveday, taking stock of the faded white and gold wall paper, the chairs covered with lilies and roses in cross-stitch, and the knick-knacks of a past generation that were scattered about on tables and mantelpiece.

A yellow damask curtain, half-festooned, divided the back drawing-room from the front in which she was seated. From the other side of this curtain there came to her the sound of voices—those of a man and a girl.

"Cut the cards again, please," said the man's voice. "Thank you. There you are again—the queen of hearts, surrounded with diamonds, and turning her back on a knave. Miss Monroe, you can't do better than make that fortune come true. Turn your back on the man who let you go without a word and—"

"Hush!" interrupted the girl with a little laugh: "I heard the next room door open—I'm sure someone came in."

The girl's laugh seemed to Loveday utterly destitute of that echo of heart-ache that in the circumstances might have been expected.

At this moment Mr. Hawke entered the room, and almost simultaneously the two young people came from the other side of the yellow curtain and crossed towards the door.

Loveday took a survey of them as they passed.

The young man—evidently "my nephew, Jack"—was a good-looking young fellow, with dark eyes and hair. The girl was small, slight and fair. She was perceptibly less at home with Jack's uncle than she was with Jack, for her manner changed and grew formal and reserved as she came face to face with him.

"We're going downstairs to have a game of billiards," said Jack, addressing Mr. Hawke, and throwing a look of curiosity at Loveday.

"Jack," said the old gentleman, "what would you say if I told you I was going to have the house re-decorated from top to bottom, and that this lady had come to advise on the matter."

This was the nearest (and most Anglicé) approach to a fabrication that Mr. Hawke would allow to pass his lips.

"Well," answered Jack promptly, "I should say, 'not before its time.' That would cover a good deal."

Then the two young people departed in company.

Loveday went straight to her work.

"I'll begin my surveying at the top of the house, and at once, if you please," she said. "Will you kindly tell one of your maids to show me through the bed-rooms? If it is possible, let that maid be the one who waits on Miss Monroe and Mrs. Hawke."

The maid who responded to Mr. Hawke's summons was in perfect harmony with the general appearance of the house. In addition, however, to being elderly and faded, she was also remarkably sour-visaged, and carried herself as if she thought that Mr. Hawke had taken a great liberty in thus commanding her attendance.

In dignified silence she showed Loveday over the topmost story, where the servants' bed-rooms were situated, and with a somewhat supercilious expression of countenance, watched her making various entries in her note-book.

In dignified silence, also, she led the way down to the second floor, where were the principal bed-rooms of the house.

"This is Miss Monroe's room," she said, as she threw back a door of one of these rooms, and then shut her lips with a snap, as if they were never going to open again.

The room that Loveday entered was, like the rest of the house, furnished in the style that prevailed in the early Victorian period. The bedstead was elaborately curtained with pink lined upholstery; the toilet-table was befrilled with muslin and tarlatan out of all likeness to a table. The one point, however, that chiefly attracted Loveday's attention was the extreme neatness that prevailed throughout the apartment—a neatness, however, that was carried out with so strict an eye to comfort and convenience that it seemed to proclaim the hand of a first-class maid. Everything in the room was, so to speak, squared to the quarter of an inch, and yet everything that a lady could require in dressing lay ready to hand. The dressing-gown lying on the back of a chair had footstool and slippers beside it. A chair stood in front of the toilet table, and on a small Japanese table to the right of the chair were placed hair-pin box, comb and brush, and hand mirror.

"This room will want money spent upon it," said Loveday, letting her eyes roam critically in all directions. "Nothing but Moorish wood-work will take off the squareness of those corners. But what a maid Miss Monroe must have. I never before saw a room so orderly and, at the same time, so comfortable."

This was so direct an appeal to conversation that the sour-visaged maid felt compelled to open her lips.

"I wait on Miss Monroe, for the present," she said snappishly; "but, to speak the truth, she scarcely requires a maid. I never before in my life had dealings with such a young lady."

"She does so much for herself, you mean—declines much assistance."

"She's like no one else I ever had to do with." (This was said even more snappishly than before.) "She not only won't be helped in dressing, but she arranges her room every day before leaving it, even to placing the chair in front of the looking glass."

"And to opening the lid of the hair-pin box, so that she may have the pins ready to her hand," added Loveday, for a moment bending over the Japanese table, with its toilet accessories.

Another five minutes were all that Loveday accorded to the inspection of this room. Then, a little to the surprise of the dignified maid, she announced her intention of completing her survey of the bed-rooms some other time, and dismissed her at the drawing-room door, to tell Mr. Hawke that she wished to see him before leaving.

Mr. Hawke, looking much disturbed and with a telegram in his hand, quickly made his appearance.

"From my wife, to say she'll be back to-night. She'll be at Waterloo in about half an hour from now," he said, holding up the brown envelope. "Now, Miss Brooke, what are we to do? I told you how much Mrs. Hawke objected to the investigation of this matter, and she is very—well—firm when she once says a thing, and—and—"

"Set your mind at rest," interrupted Loveday; "I have done all I wished to do within your walls, and the remainder of my investigation can be carried on just as well at Lynch Court or at my own private rooms."

"Done all you wished to do!" echoed Mr. Hawke in amazement; "why, you've not been an hour in the house, and do you mean to tell me you've found out anything about the necklace or the daggers?"

"Don't ask me any questions just yet; I want you to answer one or two instead. Now, can you tell me anything about any letters Miss Monroe may have written or received since she has been in your house?"

"Yes, certainly, Sir George wrote to me very strongly about her correspondence, and begged me to keep a sharp eye on it, so as to nip in the bud any attempt to communicate with Danvers. So far, however, she does not appear to have made any such attempt. She is frankness itself over her correspondence. Every letter that has come addressed to her, she has shown either to me or to my wife, and they have one and all been letters from old friends of her father's, wishing to make her acquaintance now that she is in England. With regard to letter-writing, I am sorry to say she has a marked and most peculiar objection to it. Every one of the letters she has received, my wife tells, me, remain unanswered still. She has never once been seen, since she came to the house, with a pen in her hand. And if she wrote on the sly, I don't know how she would get her letters posted—she never goes outside the door by herself, and she would have no opportunity of giving them to any of the servants to post except Mrs. Hawke's maid, and she is beyond suspicion in such a matter. She has been well cautioned, and, in addition, is not the sort of person who would assist a young lady in carrying on a clandestine correspondence."

"I should imagine not! I suppose Miss Monroe has been present at the breakfast table each time that you have received your daggers through the post—you told me, I think, that they had come by the first post in the morning?"

"Yes; Miss Monroe is very punctual at meals, and has been present each time. Naturally, when I received such unpleasant missives, I made some sort of exclamation and then handed the thing round the table for inspection, and Miss Monroe was very much concerned to know who my secret enemy could be."

"No doubt. Now, Mr. Hawke, I have a very special request to make to you, and I hope you will be most exact in carrying it out."

"You may rely upon my doing so to the very letter."

"Thank you. If, then, you should receive by post to-morrow morning one of those big envelopes you already know the look of, and find that it contains a sketch of three, not two, drawn daggers—"

"Good gracious! what makes you think such a thing likely?" exclaimed Mr. Hawke, greatly disturbed. "Why am I to be persecuted in this way? Am I to take it for granted that I am a doomed man?"

He began to pace the room in a state of great excitement.

"I don't think I would if I were you," answered Loveday calmly. "Pray let me finish. I want you to open the big envelope that may come to you by post to-morrow morning just you have opened the others—in full view of your family at the breakfast-table—and to hand round the sketch it may contain for inspection to your wife, your nephew and to Miss Monroe. Now, will you promise me to do this?"

"Oh, certainly; I should most likely have done so without any promising. But—but—I'm sure you'll understand that I feel myself to be in a peculiarly uncomfortable position, and I shall feel so very much obliged to you if you'll tell me—that is if you'll enter a little more fully into an explanation."

Loveday looked at her watch. "I should think Mrs. Hawke would be just at this moment arriving at Waterloo; I'm sure you'll be glad to see the last of me. Please come to me at my rooms in Gower Street to-morrow at twelve—here is my card. I shall then be able to enter into fuller explanations I hope. Good-bye."

The old gentleman showed her politely downstairs, and, as he shook hands with her at the front door, again asked, in a most emphatic manner, if she did not consider him to be placed in a "peculiarly unpleasant position."

Those last words at parting were to be the first with which he greeted her on the following morning when he presented himself at her rooms in Gower Street. They were, however, repeated in considerably more agitated a manner.

"Was there ever a man in a more miserable position!" he exclaimed, as he took the chair that Loveday indicated. "I not only received the three daggers for which you prepared me, but I got an additional worry, for which I was totally unprepared. This morning, immediately after breakfast, Miss Monroe walked out of the house all by herself, and no one knows where she has gone. And the girl has never before been outside the door alone. It seems the servants saw her go out, but did not think it necessary to tell either me or Mrs. Hawke, feeling sure we must have been aware of the fact."

"So Mrs. Hawke has returned," said Loveday. "Well, I suppose you will be greatly surprised if I inform you that the young lady, who has so unceremoniously left your house, is at the present moment to be found at the Charing Cross Hotel, where she has engaged a private room in her real name of Miss Mary O'Grady."

"Eh! What! Private room! Real name O'Grady! I'm all bewildered!"

"It is a little bewildering; let me explain. The young lady whom you received into your house as the daughter of your old friend, was in reality the person engaged by Miss Monroe to fulfill the duties of her maid on board ship, after her native attendant had been landed at Malta. Her real name, as I have told you, is Mary O'Grady, and she has proved herself a valuable coadjutor to Miss Monroe in assisting her to carry out a programme, which she must have arranged with her lover, Mr. Danvers, before she left Pekin."

"Eh! what!" again exclaimed Mr. Hawke; "how do you know all this? Tell me the whole story."

"I will tell you the whole story first, and then explain to you how I came to know it. From what has followed, it seems to me that Miss Monroe must have arranged with Mr. Danvers that he was to leave Pekin within ten days of her so doing, travel by the route by which she came, and land at Plymouth, where he was to receive a note from her, apprising him of her whereabouts. So soon as she was on board ship, Miss Monroe appears to have set her wits to work with great energy; every obstacle to the carrying-out of her programme she appears to have met and conquered. Step number one was to get rid of her native maid, who, perhaps, might have been faithful to her master's interests and have proved troublesome. I have no doubt the poor woman suffered terribly from sea-sickness, as it was her first voyage, and I have equally no doubt that Miss Monroe worked on her fears, and persuaded her to land at Malta, and return to China by the next packet. Step number two was to find a suitable person, who for a consideration, would be willing to play the part of the Pekin heiress among the heiress's friends in England, while the young lady herself arranged her private affairs to her own liking. That person was quickly found among the steerage passengers of the *Colombo* in Miss Mary O'Grady, who had come on board with her mother at Ceylon, and who, from the glimpse I had of her, must, I should conjecture, have been absent many years from the land of her birth. You know how cleverly this young lady has played her part in your house—how, without attracting attention to the matter, she has shunned the society of her father's old Chinese friends, who might be likely to involve her in embarrassing conversations; how she has avoided the use of pen and ink lest—"

"Yes, yes," interrupted Mr. Hawke; "but, my dear Miss Brooke, wouldn't it be as well for you and me to go at once to the Charing Cross Hotel, and get all the information we can out of her respecting Miss Monroe and her movements—she may be bolting, you know?"

CATHERINE LOUISA PIRKIS

"I do not think she will. She is waiting there patiently for an answer to a telegram she dispatched more than two hours ago to her mother, Mrs. O'Grady, at 14, Woburn Place, Cork."

"Dear me! dear me! How is it possible for you to know all this."

"Oh, that last little fact was simply a matter of astuteness on the part of the man whom I have deputed to watch the young lady's movements to-day. Other details, I assure you, in this somewhat intricate case, have been infinitely more difficult to get at. I think I have to thank those 'drawn daggers,' that caused you so much consternation, for having, in the first instance, put me on the right track."

"Ah—h," said Mr. Hawke, drawing a long breath; "now we come to the daggers! I feel sure you are going to set my mind at rest on that score."

"I hope so. Would it surprise you very much to be told that it was I who sent to you those three daggers this morning?"

"You! Is it possible?"

"Yes, they were sent by me, and for a reason that I will presently explain to you. But let me begin at the beginning. Those roughly-drawn sketches, that to you suggested terrifying ideas of blood-shedding and violence, to my mind were open to a more peaceful and commonplace explanation. They appeared to me to suggest the herald's office rather than the armoury; the cross fitchée of the knight's shield rather than the poniard with which the members of secret societies are supposed to render their recalcitrant brethren familiar. Now, if you will look at these sketches again, you will see what I mean." Here Loveday produced from her writing-table the missives which had so greatly disturbed Mr. Hawke's peace of mind. "To begin with, the blade of the dagger of common life is, as a rule, at least two-thirds of the weapon in length; in this sketch, what you would call the blade, does not exceed the hilt in length. Secondly, please note the absence of guard for the hand. Thirdly, let me draw your attention to the squareness of what you considered the hilt of the weapon, and what, to my mind, suggested the upper portion of a crusader's cross. No hand could grip such a hilt as the one outlined here. After your departure yesterday, I drove to the British Museum, and there consulted a certain valuable work on heraldry, which has more than once done me good service. There I found my surmise substantiated in a surprising manner. Among the illustrations of the various crosses borne on armorial shields, I found one that had been taken by Henri d'Anvers from his own armorial bearings, for his crest when he joined the Crusaders under Edward I., and which has since been handed down as the crest of the Danvers family. This was an important item of information to me. Here was someone in Cork sending to your house, on two several occasions, the crest of the Danvers family; with what object it would be difficult to say, unless it were in some sort a communication to someone in your house. With my mind full of this idea, I left the Museum and drove next to the office of the P. and O. Company, and requested to have given me the list of the passengers who arrived by the *Colombo*. I found this list to be a remarkably small one; I suppose people, if possible, avoid crossing the Bay of Biscay during the Equinoxes. The only passengers who landed at Plymouth besides Miss Monroe, I found, were a certain Mrs. and Miss O'Grady, steerage passengers who had gone on board at Ceylon on their way home from Australia. Their name, together with their landing at Plymouth, suggested the possibility that Cork might be their destination. After this I asked to see the list of the passengers who arrived by the packet following the *Colombo*, telling the clerk who attended to me that I was on the look-out for the arrival of a friend. In that second list of arrivals I quickly found my friend—William Wentworth Danvers by name."

"No! The effrontery! How dared he! In his own name, too!"

"Well, you see, a plausible pretext for leaving Pekin could easily be invented by him—the death of a relative, the illness of a father or mother. And Sir George, though he might dislike the idea of the young man going to England so soon after his daughter's departure, and may, perhaps, write to you by the next mail on the matter, was utterly powerless to prevent his so doing. This young man, like Miss Monroe and the O'Gradys, also landed at Plymouth. I had only arrived so far in my investigation when I went to your house yesterday afternoon. By chance, as I waited a few minutes in your drawing-room, another important item of information was acquired. A fragment of conversation between your nephew and the supposed Miss Monroe fell upon my ear, and one word spoken by the young lady convinced me of her nationality. That one word was the monosyllable 'Hush.'"

"No! You surprise me!"

"Have you never noted the difference between the 'hush' of an Englishman and that of an Irishman? The former begins his 'hush' with a distinct aspirate, the latter with as distinct a W. That W is a mark of his nationality which he never loses. The unmitigated 'whist' may lapse into a 'whish' when he is is transplanted to another soil, and the 'whish' may in course of time pass into a 'whush,' but to the distinct aspirate of the English 'hush,' he never attains. Now Miss O'Grady's was as pronounced a 'whush' as it was possible for the lips of a Hibernian to utter."

"And from that you concluded that Mary O'Grady was playing the part of Miss Monroe in my house?"

"Not immediately. My suspicions were excited, certainly; and when I went up to her room, in company with Mrs. Hawke's maid, those suspicions were confirmed. The orderliness of that room was something remarkable. Now, there is the orderliness of a lady in the arrangement of her room, and the orderliness of a maid, and the two things, believe me, are widely different. A lady, who has no maid, and who has the gift of orderliness, will put things away when done with, and so leave her room a picture of neatness. I don't think, however, it would for a moment occur to her to pull things so as to be conveniently ready for her to use the next time she dresses in that room. This would be what a maid, accustomed to arrange a room for her mistress's use, would do mechanically. Miss Monroe's room was the neatness of a maid—not of a lady, and I was assured by Mrs. Hawke's maid that it was a neatness accomplished by her own hands. As I stood there, looking at that room, the whole conspiracy—if I may so call it—little by little pieced itself together, and became plain to me. Possibilities quickly grew into probabilities, and these probabilities once admitted, brought other suppositions in their train. Now, supposing that Miss Monroe and Mary O'Grady had agreed to change places, the Pekin heiress, for the time being, occupying Mary O'Grady's place in the humble home at Cork and vice versa, what means of communicating with each other had they arranged? How was Mary O'Grady to know when she might lay aside her assumed rôle and go back to her mother's house. There was no denying the necessity for such communication; the difficulties in its way must have been equally obvious to the two girls. Now, I think we must admit that we must credit these young women with having hit upon a very clever way of meeting those difficulties. An anonymous and startling missive sent to you would be bound to be mentioned in the house, and in this way a code of signals might be set up between them that could not direct suspicion to them. In this connection, the Danvers crest, which it is possible that they mistook for a dagger, suggested itself naturally, for no doubt Miss Monroe had many impressions of it on her lover's letters. As

I thought over these things, it occurred to me that possibly dagger (or cross) number one was sent to notify the safe arrival of Miss Monroe and Mrs. O'Grady at Cork. The two daggers or crosses you subsequently received were sent on the day of Mr. Danvers's arrival at Plymouth, and were, I should say, sketched by his hand. Now, was it not within the bounds of likelihood that Miss Monroe's marriage to this young man, and the consequent release of Mary O'Grady from the onerous part she was playing, might be notified to her by the sending of three such crosses or daggers to you. The idea no sooner occurred to me than I determined to act upon it, forestall the sending of this latest communication, and watch the result. Accordingly, after I left your house yesterday, I had a sketch made of three daggers of crosses exactly similar to those you had already received, and had it posted to you so that you would get it by the first post. I told off one of our staff at Lynch Court to watch your house, and gave him special directions to follow and report on Miss O'Grady's movements throughout the day. The results I anticipated quickly came to pass. About half-past nine this morning the man sent a telegram to me from your house to the Charing Cross Hotel, and furthermore had ascertained that she had since despatched a telegram, which (possibly by following the hotel servant who carried it to the telegraph office), he had overheard was addressed to Mrs. O'Grady, at Woburn Place, Cork. Since I received this information an altogether remarkable cross-firing of telegrams has been going backwards and forwards along the wires to Cork."

"A cross-firing of telegrams! I do not understand."

"In this way. So soon as I knew Mrs. O'Grady's address I telegraphed to her, in her daughter's name, desiring her to address her reply to 1154 Gower Street, not to Charing Cross Hotel. About three-quarters of an hour afterwards I received in reply this telegram, which I am sure you will read with interest.

Here Loveday handed a telegram—one of several that lay on her writing-table—to Mr. Hawke.

He opened it and read aloud as follows:

"Am puzzled. Why such hurry? Wedding took place this morning. You will receive signal as agreed to-morrow. Better return to Tavistock Square for the night."

"The wedding took place this morning," repeated Mr. Hawke blankly. "My poor old friend! It will break his heart."

"Now that the thing is done past recall we must hope he will make the best of it," said Loveday. "In reply to this telegram," she went on, "I sent another, asking as to the movements of the bride and bridegroom, and got in reply this:"

Here she read aloud as follows:

"They will be at Plymouth to-morrow night; at Charing Cross Hotel and next day, as agreed."

"So, Mr. Hawke," she added, "if you wish to see your old friend's daughter and tell her what you think of the part she has played, all you will have to do will be to watch the arrival of the Plymouth trains."

"Miss O'Grady has called to see a lady and gentleman," said a maid at that moment entering.

"Miss O'Grady!" repeated Mr. Hawke in astonishment.

"Ah, yes, I telegraphed to her, just before you came in, to come here to meet a lady and gentlemen, and she, no doubt thinking that she would find here the newly-married pair, has, you see, lost no time in complying with my request. Show the lady in."

"It's all so intricate—so bewildering," said Mr. Hawke, as he lay back in his chair. "I can scarcely get it all into my head."

His bewilderment, however, was nothing compared with that of Miss O'Grady, when she entered the room and found herself face to face with her late guardian, instead of the radiant bride and bridegroom whom she had expected to meet.

She stood silent in the middle of the room, looking the picture of astonishment and distress.

Mr. Hawke also seemed a little at a loss for words, so Loveday took the initiative.

"Please sit down," she said, placing a chair for the girl. "Mr. Hawke and I have sent to you in order to ask you a few questions. Before doing so, however, let me tell you that the whole of your conspiracy with Miss Monroe has been brought to light, and the best thing you can do, if you want your share in it treated leniently, will be to answer our questions as fully and truthfully as possible."

The girl burst into tears. "It was all Miss Monroe's fault from beginning to end," she sobbed. "Mother didn't want to do it—I didn't want to—to go into a gentleman's house and pretend to be what I was not. And we didn't want her hundred pounds—"

Here sobs checked her speech.

"Oh," said Loveday contemptuously, "so you were to have a hundred pounds for your share in this fraud, were you?"

"We didn't want to take it," said the girl, between hysterical bursts of tears; "but Miss Monroe said if we didn't help her someone else would, and so I agreed to—"

"I think," interrupted Loveday, "that you can tell us very little that we do not already know about what you agreed to do. What we want you to tell us is what has been done with Miss Monroe's diamond necklace—who has possession of it now?"

The girl's sobs and tears redoubled. "I've had nothing to do with the necklace—it has never been in my possession," she sobbed. "Miss Monroe gave it to Mr. Danvers two or three months before she left Pekin, and he sent it on to some people he knew in Hong Kong, diamond merchants, who lent him money on it. Decastro, Miss Monroe said, was the name of these people."

"Decastro, diamond merchant, Hong Kong. I should think that would be sufficient address," said Loveday, entering it in a ledger; "and I suppose Mr. Danvers retained part of that money for his own use and travelling expenses, and handed the remainder to Miss Monroe to enable her to bribe such creatures as you and your mother, to practice a fraud that ought to land both of you in jail."

The girl grew deadly white. "Oh, don't do that—don't send us to prison!" she implored, clasping her hands together. "We haven't touched a penny of Miss Monroe's money yet, and we don't want to touch a penny, if you'll only let us off! Oh, pray, pray, pray be merciful!"

Loveday looked at Mr. Hawke.

He rose from his chair. "I think the best thing you can do," he said, "will be to get back home to your mother at Cork as quickly as possible, and advise her never to play such a risky game again. Have you any money in your purse? No—well then here's some for you, and lose no time in getting home. It will be best for Miss Monroe—Mrs. Danvers I mean—to come to my house and claim her own property there. At any rate, there it will remain until she does so."

As the girl, with incoherent expressions of gratitude, left the room, he turned to Loveday.

"I should like to have consulted Mrs. Hawke before arranging matters in this way," he said a little hesitatingly; "but still, I don't see that I could have done otherwise."

"I feel sure Mrs. Hawke will approve what you have done when she hears all the circumstance of the case," said Loveday.

"And," continued the old clergyman, "when I write to Sir George, as, of course, I must immediately, I shall advise him to make the best of a bad bargain, now that the thing is done. 'Past cure should be past care;' eh, Miss Brooke? And, think! what a narrow escape my nephew, Jack, has had!"

The Ghost of Fountain Lane

"W ill you be good enough to tell me how you procured my address?" said Miss Brooke, a little irritably. "I left strict orders that it was to be given to no one."

"I only obtained it with great difficulty from Mr. Dyer; had, in fact, to telegraph three times before I could get it," answered Mr. Clampe, the individual thus addressed. "I'm sure I'm awfully sorry to break into your holiday in this fashion, but—but pardon me if I say that it seems to be one in little more than name." Here he glanced meaningly at the newspapers, memoranda and books of reference with which the table at which Loveday sat was strewn.

She gave a little sigh.

"I suppose you are right," she answered; "it is a holiday in little more than name. I verily believe that we hard workers, after a time, lose our capacity for holiday-keeping. I thought I was pining for a week of perfect laziness and sea-breezes, and so I locked up my desk and fled. No sooner, however, do I find myself in full view of that magnificent sea-and-sky picture than I shut my eyes to it, fasten them instead on the daily papers and set my brains to work, *con amore*, on a ridiculous case that is never likely to come into my hands."

That "magnificent sea-and-sky picture" was one framed by the windows of a room on the fifth floor of the Métropole, at Brighton, whither Loveday, overtaxed in mind and body, had fled for a brief respite from hard work. Here Inspector Clampe, of the Local District Constabulary, had found her out, in order to press the claims of what seemed to him an important case upon her. He was a neat, dapper-looking man, of about fifty, with a manner less brusque and business-like than that of most men in his profession.

"Oh pray drop the ridiculous case," he said earnestly, "and set to work, '*con amore*,' upon another far from ridiculous, and most interesting."

"I'm not sure that it would interest me one quarter so much as the ridiculous one."

"Don't be sure till you've heard the particulars. Listen to this." Here the inspector took a newspaper-cutting from his pocket-book and read aloud as follows:

"'A cheque, the property of the Rev. Charles Turner, Vicar of East Downes, has been stolen under somewhat peculiar circumstances. It appears that the Rev. gentleman was suddenly called from home by the death of a relative, and thinking he might possibly be away some little time, he left with his wife four blank cheques, signed, for her to fill in as required. They were made payable to self or bearer, and were drawn on the West Sussex Bank. Mrs. Turner, when first questioned on the matter, stated that as soon as her husband had departed, she locked up these cheques in her writing desk. She subsequently, however, corrected this statement, and admitted having left them on the table while she went into the garden to cut some flowers. In all, she was absent, she says, about ten minutes. When she came in from cutting her flowers, she immediately put the cheques away. She had not counted them on receiving them from her husband, and when, as she put them into her Davenport, she saw there were only three, she concluded that that was the number he had left with her. The loss of the cheque was not discovered until her husband's return, about a week later on. As soon as he was aware of the fact, he telegraphed to the West Sussex Bank to stop payment, only, however, to make the unpleasant discovery that the cheque, filled in to the amount of six hundred pounds, had been presented and cashed (in gold) two days previously. The clerk who cashed it took no particular notice of the person presenting it, except that he was of gentlemanly appearance, and declares himself to be quite incapable of identifying him. The largeness of the amount raised no suspicion in the mind of the clerk, as Mr. Turner is a man of good means, and since his marriage, about six months back, has been refurnishing the Vicarage, and paying away large sums for old oak furniture and for pictures.'"

"There, Miss Brooke," said the inspector as he finished reading, "if, in addition to these particulars, I tell you that one or two circumstances that have arisen seem to point suspicion in the direction of the young wife, I feel sure you will admit that a more interesting case, and one more worthy of your talents, is not to be found."

Loveday's answer was to take up a newspaper that lay beside her on the table. "So much for your interesting case," she said; "now listen to my ridiculous one." Then she read aloud as follows:—

"'Authentic Ghost Story.—The inhabitants of Fountain Lane, a small turning leading off Ship Street, have been greatly disturbed by the sudden appearance of a ghost in their midst. Last Tuesday night, between ten and eleven o'clock, a little girl named Martha Watts, who lives as a help to a shoemaker and his wife at No. 5 in the lane, ran out into the streets in her night-clothes in a great state of terror, saying that a ghost had come to her bedside. The child refused to return to the house to sleep, and was accordingly taken in by some neighbours. The shoemaker and his wife, Freer by name, when questioned by the neighbours on the matter, admitted, with great reluctance, that they, too, had seen the apparition, which they described as being a soldier-like individual, with a broad, white forehead and having his arms folded on his breast. This description is, in all respects confirmed by the child, Martha Watts, who asserts that the ghost she saw reminded her of pictures she had seen of the great Napoleon. The Freers state that it first appeared in the course of a prayer-meeting held at their house on the previous night, when it was distinctly seen by Mr. Freer. Subsequently, the wife, awakening suddenly in the middle of the night, saw the apparition standing at the foot of the bed. They are quite at a loss for an explanation of the matter. The affair has caused quite a sensation in the district, and at the time of going to press, the lane is so thronged and crowded by would-be ghost-seers that the inhabitants have great difficulty in going to and from their houses.'"

"A scare—a vulgar scare, nothing more," said the inspector as Loveday laid aside the paper. "Now, Miss Brooke, I ask you seriously, supposing you get to the bottom of such a stupid, commonplace fraud as that, will you in any way add to your reputation?"

"And supposing I get to the bottom of such a stupid, commonplace fraud as a stolen cheque, how much, I should like to know, do I add to my reputation?"

"Well, put it on other grounds and allow Christian charity to have some claims. Think of the misery in that gentleman's house unless suspicion can be lifted from the young wife and directed to the proper quarter."

"Think of the misery of the landlord of the Fountain Lane houses if all his tenants decamp in a body, as they no doubt will, unless the ghost mystery is solved."

The inspector sighed. "Well, I suppose I must take it for granted that you will have nothing to do with the case," he said. "I brought the cheque with me, thinking you might like to see it."

"I suppose it's very much like other cheques?" said Loveday indifferently, and turning over her memoranda as if she meant to go back to her ghost again.

"Ye—es," said Mr. Clampe, taking the cheque from his pocket-book and glancing down at it. "I suppose the cheque is very much like other cheques. This little scribble of figures in pencil at the back—144,000— can scarcely be called a distinguishing mark."

"What's that, Mr. Clampe?" asked Loveday, pushing her memoranda on one side. "144,000 did you say?"

Her whole manner had suddenly changed from apathy to that of keenest interest.

Mr. Clampe, delighted, rose and spread the cheque before her on the table.

"The writing of the words "six hundred pounds," he said, "bears so close a resemblance to Mr. Turner's signature, that the gentleman himself told me he would have thought it was his own writing if he had not known that he had not drawn a cheque for that amount on the given date. You see it is that round, school-boy's hand, so easy to imitate, I could write it myself with half-an-hour's practice; no flourishes, nothing distinctive about it."

Loveday made no reply. She had turned the cheque, and was now closely scrutinizing the pencilled figures at the back.

"Of course," continued the inspector, "those figures were not written by the person who wrote the figures on the face of the cheque. That, however, matters but little. I really do not think they are of the slightest importance in the case. They might have been scribbled by some one making a calculation as to the number of pennies in six hundred pounds—there are, as no doubt you know, exactly 144,000."

"Who has engaged your services in this case, the Bank or Mr. Turner?"

"Mr. Turner. When the loss of the cheque was first discovered, he was very excited and irate, and when he came to me the day before yesterday, I had much difficulty in persuading him that there was no need to telegraph to London for half-a-dozen detectives, as we could do the work quite as well as the London men. When, however, I went over to East Downes yesterday to look round and ask a few questions; I found things had altogether changed. He was exceedingly reluctant to answer any questions, lost his temper when I pressed them, and as good as told me that he wished he had not moved in the matter at all. It was this sudden change of demeanour that turned my thoughts in the direction of Mrs. Turner. A man must have a very strong reason for wishing to sit idle under a loss of six hundred pounds, for, of course, under the circumstances, the Bank will not bear the brunt of it."

"Some other motives may be at work in his mind, consideration for old servants, the wish to avoid a scandal in the house."

"Quite so. The fact, taken by itself, would give no ground for suspicion, but certainly looks ugly if taken in connection with another fact which I have since ascertained, namely, that during her husband's absence from home, Mrs. Turner paid off certain debts contracted by her in Brighton before the marriage, and amounting to nearly £500. Paid them off, too, in gold. I think I mentioned to you that the gentleman who presented the stolen cheque at the Bank preferred payment in gold."

"You are supposing not only a confederate, but also a vast amount of cunning as well as of simplicity on the lady's part."

"Quite so. Three parts cunning to one of simplicity is precisely what lady criminals are composed of. And it is, as a rule, that one part of simplicity that betrays them and leads to their detection."

"What sort of woman is Mrs. Turner in other respects?"

"She is young, handsome and of good birth, but is scarcely suited for the position of vicar's wife in a country parish. She has lived a good deal in society and is fond of gaiety, and, in addition, is a Roman Catholic, and, I am told, utterly ignores her husband's church and drives every Sunday to Brighton to attend mass."

"WHAT ABOUT THE SERVANTS IN the house? Do they seem steady-going and respectable?"

"There was nothing on the surface to excite suspicion against any one of them. But it is precisely in that quarter than your services would be invaluable. It will, however, be impossible to get you inside the vicarage walls. Mr. Turner, I am confident, would never open his doors to you."

"What do you suggest?"

"I can suggest nothing better than the house of the village schoolmistress, or, rather, of the village schoolmistress's mother, Mrs. Brown. It is only a stone's throw from the vicarage; in fact, its windows overlook the vicarage grounds. It is a four-roomed cottage, and Mrs. Brown, who is a very respectable person, turns over a little money in the summer by receiving lady lodgers desirous of a breath of country air. There would be no difficulty in getting you in there; her spare bedroom is empty now."

"I should have preferred being at the vicarage, but if it cannot be, I must make the most of my stay at Mrs. Brown's. How do we get there?'"

"I drove from East Downes here in a trap I hired at the village inn where I put up last night, and where I shall stay to-night. I will drive you, if you will allow me; it is only seven miles off. It's a lovely day for a drive; breezy and not too much dust. Could you be ready in about half an hour's time, say?"

But this, Loveday said, would be an impossibility. She had a special engagement that afternoon; there was a religious service in the town that she particularly wished to attend. It would not be over until three o'clock, and, consequently, not until half-past three would she be ready for the drive to East Downes.

Although Mr. Clampe looked unutterable astonishment at the claims of a religious service being set before those of professional duty, he made no demur to the arrangement, and accordingly half-past three saw Loveday and the inspector in a high-wheeled dog-cart rattling along the Marina in the direction of East Downes.

Loveday made no further allusion to her ghost story, so Mr. Clampe, out of politeness, felt compelled to refer to it.

"I heard all about the Fountain Lane ghost yesterday, before I started for East Downes," he said; "and it seemed to me, with all deference to you, Miss Brooke, an every-day sort of affair, the sort of thing to be explained by a heavy supper or an extra glass of beer."

"There are a few points in this ghost story that separate it from the every-day ghost story," answered Loveday. "For instance, you would expect that such emotionally religious people, as I have since found the Freers to be, would have seen a vision of angels, or at least a solitary saint. Instead, they see a soldier! A soldier, too, in the likeness of a man who is anathema maranatha to every religious mind—the great Napoleon."

"To what denomination do the Freers belong?"

"To the Wesleyan. Their fathers and mothers before them were Wesleyans; their relatives and friends are Wesleyans, one and all, they say; and, most important item of all, the man's boot and shoe connection lies exclusively among Wesleyan ministers. This, he told me, is the most paying connection that a small boot-maker can have. Half-a-dozen Wesleyan ministers pay better than three times the number of Church clergy, for whereas the Wesleyan minister is always on the tramp among his people, the clergyman generally contrives in the country to keep a horse, or else turns student, and shuts himself up in his study."

"Ha, ha! Capital," laughed Mr. Clampe; "tell that to the Church Defence Society in Wales. Isn't this a first-rate little horse? In another ten minutes we shall be in sight of East Downes."

The long, dusty road down which they had driven, was ending now in a narrow, sloping lane, hedged in on either side with hawthorns and wild plum trees. Through these, the August sunshine was beginning to slant now, and from a distant wood there came a faint sound of fluting and piping, as if the blackbirds were thinking of tuning up for their evening carols.

A sudden, sharp curve in this lane brought them in sight of East Downes, a tiny hamlet of about thirty cottages, dominated by the steeple of a church of early English architecture. Adjoining the church was the vicarage, a goodly-sized house, with extensive grounds, and in a lane running alongside these grounds were situated the village schools and the schoolmistress's house. The latter was simply a four-roomed cottage, standing in a pretty garden, with cluster roses and honeysuckle, now in the fullness of their August glory, climbing upwards to its very roof.

Outside this cottage Mr. Clampe drew rein.

"If you'll give me five minutes' grace," he said, "I'll go in and tell the good woman that I have brought her, as a lodger, a friend of mine, who is anxious to get away for a time from the noise and glare of Brighton. Of course, the story of the stolen cheque is all over the place, but I don't think anyone has, at present, connected me with the affair. I am supposed to be a gentleman from Brighton, who is anxious to buy a horse the Vicar wishes to sell, and who can't quite arrange terms with him."

While Loveday waited outside in the cart, an open carriage drove past and then in through the vicarage gates. In the carriage were seated a gentleman and lady whom, from the respectful greetings they received from the village children, she conjectured to be the Rev. Charles and Mrs. Turner. Mr. Turner was sanguine-complexioned, red-haired, and wore a distinctly troubled expression of countenance. With Mrs. Turner's appearance Loveday was not favourably impressed. Although a decidedly handsome woman, she was hard-featured and had a scornful curl to her upper lip. She was dressed in the extreme of London fashion.

They threw a look of enquiry at Loveday as they passed, and she felt sure that enquiries as to the latest addition to Mrs. Brown's ménage would soon be afloat in the village.

Mr. Clampe speedily returned, saying that Mrs. Brown was only too delighted to get her spare-room occupied. He whispered a hint as they made their way up to the cottage door between borders thickly planted with stocks and mignonette.

It was:

"Don't ask her any questions, or she'll draw herself up as straight as a ramrod, and say she never listens to gossip of any sort. But just let her alone, and she'll run on like a mill-stream, and tell you as much as you'll want to know about everyone and everything. She and the village postmistress are great friends, and between them they contrive to know pretty much what goes on inside every house in the place."

Mrs. Brown was a stout, rosy-cheeked woman of about fifty, neatly dressed in a dark stuff gown with a big white cap and apron. She welcomed Loveday respectfully, and introduced, evidently with a little pride, her daughter, the village schoolmistress, a well-spoken young woman of about eight-and-twenty.

Mr. Clampe departed with his dog-cart to the village inn, announcing his intention of calling on Loveday at the cottage on the following morning before he returned to Brighton.

Miss Brown also departed, saying she would prepare tea. Left alone with Loveday, Mrs. Brown speedily unloosed her tongue. She had a dozen questions to ask respecting Mr. Clampe and his business in the village. Now, was it true that he had come to East Downes for the whole and sole purpose of buying one of the Vicar's horses? She had heard it whispered that he had been sent by the police to watch the servants at the vicarage. She hoped it was not true, for a more respectable set of servants were not to be met with in any house, far or near. Had Miss Brooke heard about that lost cheque? Such a terrible affair! She had been told that the story of it had reached London. Now, had Miss Brooke seen an account of it in any of the London papers?

Here a reply from Loveday in the negative formed a sufficient excuse for relating with elaborate detail the story of the stolen cheque. Except in its elaborateness of detail, it differed but little from the one Loveday had already heard.

She listened patiently, bearing in mind Mr. Clampe's hint, and asking no questions. And when, in about a quarter of an hour's time, Miss Brown came in with the tea-tray in her hand, Loveday could have passed an examination in the events of the daily family life at the vicarage. She could have answered questions as to the ill-assortedness of the newly-married couple; she knew that they wrangled from morning till night; that the chief subjects of their disagreement were religion and money matters; that the Vicar was hot-tempered, and said whatever came to the tip of his tongue; that the beautiful young wife, though slower of speech, was scathing and sarcastic, and that, in addition, she was wildly extravagant and threw money away in all directions.

In addition to these interesting facts, Loveday could have undertaken to supply information respecting the number of servants at the vicarage, together with their names, ages and respective duties.

During tea, conversation flagged somewhat; Miss Brown's presence evidently acted repressively on her mother, and it was not until the meal was over and Loveday was being shown to her room by Mrs. Brown that opportunity to continue the talk was found.

Loveday opened the ball by remarking on the fact that no Dissenting chapel was to be found in the village.

"Generally, wherever there is a handful of cottages, we find a church at one end and a chapel at the other," she said; "but here, willy-nilly, one must go to church."

"Do you belong to chapel, ma'am?" was Mrs. Brown's reply. "Old Mrs. Turner, the Vicar's mother, who died over a year ago, was so 'low' she was almost chapel, and used often to drive over to Brighton to attend the Countess of Huntingdon's church. People used to say that was bad enough in the Vicar's mother; but what was it compared with what goes on now—the Vicar's wife driving regularly every Sunday into Brighton to a Catholic Church to say her prayers to candles and images? I'm glad you like the room, ma'am. Feather bolster, feather pillows, do you see, ma'am? I've nothing in the way of flock or wool on either of my beds to make people's head ache." Here Mrs. Brown, by way of emphasis, patted and pinched the fat pillows and bolster showing above the spotless white counterpane.

Loveday stood at the cottage window drinking in the sweetness of the country air, laden now with the heavy evening scents of carnation and essamine. Across the road, from the vicarage, came the loud clanging of a dinner-gong, and almost simultaneously the church clock chimed the hour—seven o'clock.

"Who is that person coming up the lane?" asked Loveday, her attention suddenly attracted by a tall, thin figure, dressed in shabby black, with a large, dowdyish bonnet, and carrying a basket in her hand as if she were returning from some errand. Mrs. Brown peeped over Loveday's shoulder.

"Ah, that's the peculiar young woman I was telling you about, ma'am—Maria Lisle, who used to be old Mrs. Turner's maid. Not that she is over young now; she's five-and-thirty if she's a day. The Vicar kept her on to be his wife's maid after the old lady died, but young Mrs. Turner will have nothing to do with her, she's not good enough for her; so Mr. Turner is just paying her £30 a year for doing nothing. And what Maria does with all that money it would be hard to say. She doesn't spend it on dress, that's certain, and she hasn't kith nor kin, not a soul belonging to her to give a penny to."

"Perhaps she gives it to charities in Brighton. There are plenty of outlets for money there."

"She may," said Mrs. Brown dubiously; "she is always going to Brighton whenever she gets a chance. She used to be a Wesleyan in old Mrs. Turner's time, and went regularly to all the revival meetings for miles round; what she is now, it would be hard to say. Where she goes to church in Brighton, no one knows. She drives over with Mrs. Turner every Sunday, but everyone knows nothing would induce her to go near the candles and images. Thomas—that's the coachman—says he puts her down at the corner of a dirty little street in mid-Brighton, and there he picks her up again after he has fetched Mrs. Turner from her church. No, there's something very queer in her ways."

Maria passed in through the lodge gates of the vicarage. She walked with her head bent, her eyes cast down to the ground.

"Something very queer in her ways," repeated Mrs. Brown. "She never speaks to a soul unless they speak first to her, and gets by herself on every possible opportunity. Do you see that old summer-house over there in the vicarage grounds—it stands between the orchard and kitchen garden—well, every evening at sunset, out comes Maria and disappears into it, and there she stays for over an hour at a time. And what she does there goodness only knows!"

"Perhaps she keeps books there, and studies."

"Studies! My daughter showed her some new books that had come down for the fifth standard the other day, and Maria turned upon her and said quite sharply that there was only one book in the whole world that people ought to study, and that book was the Bible."

"How pretty those vicarage gardens are," said Loveday, a little abruptly. "Does the Vicar ever allow people to see them?"

"Oh, yes, miss; he doesn't at all mind people taking a walk round them. Only yesterday he said to me, 'Mrs. Brown, if ever you feel yourself circumscribed'—yes, 'circumscribed' was the word—'just walk out of your garden-gate and in at mine and enjoy yourself at your leisure among my fruit-trees.' Not that I would like to take advantage of his kindness and make too free; but if you'd care, ma'am, to go for a walk through the grounds, I'll go with you with pleasure. There's a wonderful old cedar hard by the pond people have come ever so far to see."

"It's that old summer-house and little bit of orchard that fascinate me," said Loveday, putting on her hat.

"We shall frighten Maria to death if she sees us so near her haunt," said Mrs. Brown as she led the way downstairs. "This way, if you please, ma'am, the kitchen-garden leads straight into the orchard."

Twilight was deepening rapidly into night now. Bird notes had ceased, the whirr of insects, the croaking of a distant frog were the only sounds that broke the evening stillness.

As Mrs. Brown swung back the gate that divided the kitchen-garden from the orchard, the gaunt, black figure of Maria Lisle was seen approaching in an opposite direction.

"Well, really, I don't see why she should expect to have the orchard all to herself every evening," said Mrs. Brown, with a little toss of her head. "Mind the gooseberry bushes, ma'am, they do catch at your clothes so. My word! what a fine show of fruit the Vicar has this year! I never saw pear trees more laden!"

They were now in the "bit of orchard" to be seen from the cottage windows. As they rounded the corner of the path in which the old summer-house stood, Maria Lisle turned its corner at the farther end, and suddenly found herself almost face to face with them. If her eyes and not been so persistently fastened on the ground, she would have noted the approach of the intruders as quickly as they had noted hers. Now, as she saw them for the first time, she gave a sudden start, paused for a moment irresolutely, and then turned sharply and walked rapidly away in an opposite direction.

"Maria, Maria!" called Mrs. Brown, "don't run away; we sha'n't stay here for more than a minute or so."

Her words met with no response. The woman did not so much as turn her head.

Loveday stood at the entrance of the old summer-house. It was considerably out of repair, and most probably was never entered by anyone save Maria Lisle, its unswept, undusted condition suggesting colonies of spiders and other creeping things within.

Loveday braved them all and took her seat on the bench that ran round the little place in a semi-circle.

"Do try and overtake the girl, and tell her we shall be gone in a minute," she said, addressing Mrs. Brown. "I will wait here meanwhile. I am so sorry to have frightened her away in that fashion."

Mrs. Brown, under protest, and with a little grumble at the ridiculousness of "people who couldn't look other people in the face," set off in pursuit of Maria.

It was getting dim inside the summer-house now. There was, however, sufficient light to enable Loveday to discover a small packet of books lying in a corner of the bench on which she sat.

One by one she took them in her hand and closely scrutinized them. The first was a much read and pencil-marked Bible; the others were respectively, a "congregational hymn-book," a book in a paper cover, on which was printed a flaming picture of a red and yellow angel, pouring blood and fire from out a big black bottle, and entitled "The End of the Age," and a smaller book, also in a paper cover, on which was depicted a huge black horse, snorting fire and brimstone into ochre-coloured clouds. This book was entitled "The Year Book of the Saints," and was simply a ruled diary with sensational mottoes for every day in the year. In parts, this diary was filled in with large and very untidy handwriting.

In these books seemed to lie the explanation of Maria Lisle's love of evening solitude and the lonely old summer-house.

Mrs. Brown pursued Maria to the servants' entrance to the house, but could not overtake her, the girl making good her retreat there.

She returned to Loveday a little hot, a little breathless and a little out of temper. It was all so absurd, she said; why couldn't the woman have stayed and had a chat with them? It wasn't as if she would get any harm out of the talk; she knew as well as everyone else in the village that she (Mrs. Brown) was no idle gossip, tittle-tattling over other people's affairs.

But here Loveday, a little sharply, cut short her meanderings.

"Mrs. Brown," she said, and to Mrs. Brown's fancy her voice and manner had entirely changed from that of the pleasant, chatty lady of half-an-hour ago, "I'm sorry to say it will be impossible for me to stay even one night in your pleasant home, I have just recollected some important business that I must transact in Brighton to-night. I haven't unpacked my portmanteau, so if you'll kindly have it taken to your garden-gate, I'll call for it as we drive past—I am going now, at once, to the inn, to see if Mr. Clampe can drive me back into Brighton to-night."

Mrs. Brown had no words ready wherewith to express her astonishment, and Loveday assuredly gave her no time to hunt for them. Ten minutes later saw her rousing Mr. Clampe from a comfortable supper, to which he had just settled himself, with the surprising announcement that she must get back to Brighton with as little delay as possible; now, would he be good enough to drive her there?

"We'll have a pair if they are to be had," she added. "The road is good; it will be moonlight in a quarter of an hour; we ought to do it in less than half the time we took coming."

While a phaeton and pair were being got ready, Loveday had time for a few words of explanation.

Maria Lisle's diary in the old summer-house had given her the last of the links in her chain of evidence that was to bring the theft of the cheque home to the criminal.

"It will be best to drive straight to the police station," she said; "they must take out three warrants, one for Maria Lisle, and two others respectively for Richard Steele, late Wesleyan minister of a chapel in Gordon Street, Brighton, and John Rogers, formerly elder of the same chapel. And let me tell you," she added with a little smile, "that these three worthies would most likely have been left at large to carry on their depredations for some little time to come if it had not been for that ridiculous ghost in Fountain Lane."

More than this there was not time to add, and when, a few minutes later, the two were rattling along the road to Brighton, the presence of the man, whom they were forced to take with them in order to bring back the horses to East Downes, prevented any but the most jerky and fragmentary of additions to this brief explanation.

"I very much fear that John Rogers has bolted," once Loveday whispered under her breath.

And again, a little later, when a smooth bit of road admitted of low-voiced talk, she said:

"We can't wait for the warrant for Steele; they must follow us with it to 15, Draycott Street."

"But I want to know about the ghost," said Mr. Clampe; "I am deeply interested in that 'ridiculous ghost.'"

"Wait till we get to 15, Draycott Street," was Loveday's reply; "when you've been there, I feel sure you will understand everything."

Church clocks were chiming a quarter to nine as they drove through Kemp Town at a pace that made the passers-by imagine they must be bound on an errand of life and death.

Loveday did not alight at the police station, and five minutes' talk with the inspector in charge there was all that Mr. Clampe required to put things en train for the arrest of the three criminals.

It had evidently been an "excursionists' day" at Brighton. The streets leading to the railway station were thronged, and their progress along the bye streets was impeded by the overflow of traffic from the main road.

"We shall get along better on foot; Draycott Street is only a stone's throw from here," said Loveday; "there's a turning on the north side of Western Road that will bring us straight into it."

So they dismissed their trap, and Loveday, acting as cicerone still, led the way through narrow turnings into the district, half town, half country, that skirts the road leading to the Dyke.

Draycott Street was not difficult to find. It consisted of two rows of newly-built houses of the eight-roomed, lodging-letting order. A dim light shone from the first-floor windows of number fifteen, but the lower window was dark and uncurtained, and a board hanging from its balcony rails proclaimed that it was "to let unfurnished." The door of the house stood slightly ajar, and pushing it open, Loveday led the way up a flight of stairs—lighted halfway up with a paraffin lamp—to the first floor.

"I know the way. I was here this afternoon," she whispered to her companion. "This is the last lecture he will give before he starts for Judaea; or, in other words, bolts with the money he has managed to conjure from other people's purses into his own."

The door of the room for which they were making, on the first floor, stood open, possibly on account of the heat. It laid bare to view a double row of forms, on which were seated some eight or ten persons in the attitude of all-absorbed listeners. Their faces were upturned, as if fixed on a preacher at the farther end of the room, and wore that expression of rapt, painful interest that is sometimes seen on the faces of a congregation of revivalists before the smouldering excitement bursts into flame.

As Loveday and her companion mounted the last of the flight of stairs, the voice of the preacher—full, arrestive, resonant—fell upon their ear; and, standing on the small outside landing, it was possible to catch a glimpse of that preacher through the crack of the half-opened door.

He was a tall, dignified-looking man, of about five-and-forty, with a close crop of white hair, black eye-brows and remarkably luminous and expressive eyes. Altogether his appearance matched his voice: it was emphatically that of a man born to sway, lead, govern the multitude.

A boy came out of an adjoining room and asked Loveday respectfully if she would not like to go in and hear the lecture. She shook her head.

"I could not stand the heat," she said. "Kindly bring us chairs here."

The lecture was evidently drawing to a close now, and Loveday and Mr. Clampe, as they sat outside listening, could not resist an occasional thrill of admiration at the skilful manner in which the preacher led his hearers from one figure of rhetoric to another, until the oratorical climax was reached.

"That man is a born orator," whispered Loveday; "and in addition to the power of the voice has the power of the eye. That audience is as completely hypnotized by him as if they had surrendered themselves to a professional mesmerist."

To judge from the portion of the discourse that fell upon their ear, the preacher was a member of one of the many sects known under the generic name, "Millenarian." His topic was Apollyon and the great battle of Armageddon. This he described as vividly as if it were being fought out under his very eye, and it would scarcely be an exaggeration to say that he made the cannon roar in the ears of his listeners and the tortured cries of the wounded wail in them. He drew an appalling picture of the carnage of that battlefield, of the blood flowing like a river across the plain, of the mangled men and horses, with the birds of prey swooping down from all quarters, and the stealthy tigers and leopards creeping out from their mountain lairs. "And all this time," he said, suddenly raising his voice from a whisper to a full, thrilling tone, "gazing calmly down upon the field of slaughter, with bent brows and folded arms, stands the imperial Apollyon. Apollyon did I say? No, I will give him his right name, the name in which he will stand revealed in that dread day, Napoleon! A Napoleon it will be who, in that day, will stand as the embodiment of Satanic majesty. Out of the mists suddenly he will walk, a tall, dark figure, with frowning brows and firm-set lips. A man to rule, a man to drive, a man to kill! Apollyon the mighty, Napoleon the imperial, they are one and the same—"

Here a sob and a choking cry from one of the women in the front seats interrupted the discourse and sent the small boy who acted as verger into the room with a glass of water.

CATHERINE LOUISA PIRKIS

"That sermon has been preached before," said Loveday. "Now can you not understand the origin of the ghost in Fountain Lane?"

"Hysterics are catching, there's another woman off now," said Mr. Clampe; "it's high time this sort of thing was put a stop to. Pearson ought to be here in another minute with his warrant."

The words had scarcely passed his lips before heavy steps mounting the stairs announced that Pearson and his warrant were at hand.

"I don't think I can be of any further use," said Loveday, rising to depart. "If you like to come to me to-morrow morning at my hotel at ten o'clock I will tell you, step by step, how I came to connect a stolen cheque with a 'ridiculous ghost.'"

"We had a tussle—he showed fight at first," said Mr. Clampe, when, precisely at ten o'clock the next morning, he called upon Miss Brooke at the Métropole. "If he had had time to get his wits together and had called some of the men in that room to the rescue, I verily believe we should have been roughly handled and he might have slipped through our fingers after all. It's wonderful what power these 'born orators,' as you call them, have over minds of a certain order."

"Ah, yes," answered Loveday thoughtfully; "we talk glibly enough about 'magnetic influence,' but scarcely realize how literally true the phrase is. It is my firm opinion that the 'leaders of men,' as they are called, have as absolute and genuine hypnotic power as any modern French expert, although perhaps it may be less consciously exercised. Now tell me about Rogers and Maria Lisle."

"Rogers had bolted, as you expected he would have done, with the six hundred pounds he had been good enough to cash for his reverend colleague. Ostensibly he had started for Judea to collect the elect, as he phrased it, under one banner. In reality, he has sailed for New York, where, thanks to the cable, he will be arrested on his arrival and sent back by return packet. Maria Lisle was arrested this morning on a charge of having stolen the cheque from Mrs. Turner. By the way, Miss Brooke, I think it is almost a pity you didn't take possession of her diary when you had the chance. It would have been invaluable evidence against her and her rascally colleagues."

"I did not see the slightest necessity for so doing. Remember, she is not one of the criminal classes, but a religious enthusiast, and when put upon her defence will at once confess and plead religious conviction as an extenuating circumstance—at least, if she is well advised she will do so. I never read anything that laid bare more frankly than did this diary the mischief that the sensational teaching of these millenarians is doing at the present moment. But I must not take up your time with moralizing. I know you are anxious to learn what, in the first instance, led me to identify a millenarian preacher with a receiver of stolen property."

"Yes, that's it; I want to know about the ghost; that's the point that interests me."

"Very well. As I told you yesterday afternoon, the first thing that struck me as remarkable in this ghost story was the soldierly character of the ghost. One expects emotionally religious people like Freer and his wife to see visions, but one also expects those visions to partake of the nature of those emotions, and to be somewhat shadowy and ecstatic. It seemed to me certain that this Napoleonic ghost must have some sort of religious significance to these people. This conviction it was that set my thoughts running in the direction of the millenarians, who have attached a religious significance (although not a polite one) to the name of Napoleon by embodying the evil Apollyon in the person of a descendant of the great Emperor, and endowing him with all the qualities of his illustrious ancestor. I called upon the Freers, ordered a pair of boots, and while the man was taking my measure, I asked him a few very pointed questions on these millenarian notions. The man prevaricated a good deal at first, but at length was driven to admit that he and his wife were millenarians at heart, that, in fact, the prayer meeting at which the Napoleonic ghost had made its first appearance was a millenarian one, held by a man who had at one time been a Wesleyan preacher in the chapel in Gordon Street, but who had been dismissed from his charge there because his teaching had been held to be unsound. Freer further stated that this man had been so much liked that many members of the congregation seized every opportunity that presented itself of attending his ministrations, some openly, others, like himself and his wife, secretly, lest they might give offence to the elders and ministers of their chapel."

"And the bootmaking connection suffer proportionately," laughed Mr. Clampe.

"Precisely. A visit to the Wesleyan chapel in Gordon Street and a talk with the chapel attendant enabled me to complete the history of this inhibited preacher, the Rev. Richard Steele. From this attendant I ascertained that a certain elder of their chapel, John Rogers by name, had seceded from their communion, thrown in his lot with Richard Steele, and that the two together were now going about the country preaching that the world would come to an end on Thursday, April 11th, 1901, and that five years before this event, viz., on the 5th of March, 1896 one hundred and forty-four thousand living saints would be caught up to heaven. They furthermore announced that this translation would take place in the land of Judaea, that, shortly, saints from all parts of the world would be hastening thither, and that in view of this event a society had been formed to provide homes—a series, I suppose—for the multitudes who would otherwise be homeless. Also (a very vital point this), that subscriptions for this society would be gladly received by either gentleman. I had arrived so far in my ghost enquiry when you came to me, bringing the stolen cheque with its pencilled figures, 144,000."

"Ah, I begin to see!" murmured Mr. Clampe.

"It immediately occurred to me that the man who could make persons see an embodiment of his thought at will, would have very little difficulty in influencing other equally receptive minds to a breach of the ten commandments. The world, it seems to me, abounds in people who are little more than blank sheets of paper, on which a strong hand may transcribe what it will—hysteric subjects, the doctors would call them; hypnotic subjects others would say; really the line that divides the hysteric condition from the hypnotic is a very hazy one. So now, when I saw your stolen cheque, I said to myself, 'there is a sheet of blank paper somewhere in that country vicarage, the thing is to find it out.'"

"Ah, good Mrs. Brown's gossip made your work easy to you there."

"It did. She not only gave me a complete summary of the history of the people within the vicarage walls, but she put so many graphic touches to that history that they lived and moved before me. For instance, she told me that Maria Lisle was in the habit of speaking of Mrs. Turner as a 'Child of the Scarlet Woman,' a 'Daughter of Babylon,' and gave me various other minute particulars, which enabled me, so to speak, to see Maria Lisle going about her daily duties, rendering her mistress reluctant service, hating her in her heart as a member of a corrupt faith, and thinking she was doing God service by despoiling her of some of her wealth, in order to devote it to what seemed to her a holy cause. I would like here to read to you two entries which I copied from her diary under dates respectively, August 3rd (the day the cheque was lost), and August 7th (the following Sunday), when Maria no doubt found opportunity to meet Steele at some prayer-meeting in Brighton."

Here Loveday produced her note-book and read from it as follows:

"'To-day I have spoiled the Egyptians! Taken from a Daughter of Babylon that which would go to increase the power of the Beast!'

"And again, under date August 7th, she writes:

"'I have handed to-day to my beloved pastor that of which I despoiled at Daughter of Babylon. It was blank, but he told me he would fill it in so that 144,000 of the elect would be each the richer by one penny. Blessed thought! this is the doing of my most unworthy hand.'

"A wonderful farrago, that diary of distorted Scriptural phraseology—wild eulogies on the beloved pastor, and morbid ecstatics, such as one would think could be the outcome only of a diseased brain. It seems to me that Portland or Broadmoor, and the ministrations of a sober-minded chaplain, may be about the happiest thing that could befall Maria Lisle at this period of her career. I think I ought to mention in this connection that when at the religious service yesterday afternoon (to attend which I slightly postponed my drive to East Downes), I heard Steele pronounce a fervid eulogy on those who had strengthened his hands for the fight which he knew it would shortly fall to his lot to wage against Apollyon, I did not wonder at weak-minded persons like Maria Lisle, swayed by such eloquence, setting up new standards of right and wrong for themselves."

"Miss Brooke, another question or two. Can you in any way account for the sudden payment of Mrs. Turner's debts—a circumstance that led me a little astray in the first instance?"

"Mrs. Brown explained the matter easily enough. She said that a day or two back, when she was walking on the other side of the vicarage hedge, and the husband and wife in the garden were squabbling as usual over money-matters, she heard Mr. Turner say indignantly, 'only a week or two ago I gave you nearly £500 to pay your debts in Brighton, and now there comes another bill.'"

"Ah, that makes it plain enough. One more question and I have done. I have no doubt there's something in your theory of the hypnotic power (unconsciously exercised) of such men as Richard Steele, although, at the same time, it seems to me a trifle far-fetched and fanciful. But even admitting it, I don't see how you account for the girl, Martha Watts, seeing the ghost. She was not present at the prayer-meeting which called the ghost into being, nor does she appear in any way to have come into contact with the Rev. Richard Steele."

"Don't you think that ghost-seeing is quite as catching as scarlet-fever or measles?" answered Loveday, with a little smile. "Let one member of a family see a much individualized and easily described ghost, such as the one these good people saw, and ten to one others in the same house will see it before the week is over. We are all in the habit of asserting that 'seeing is believing.' Don't you think the converse of the saying is true also, and that 'believing is seeing?'

Missing!

N ow, Miss Brooke, if this doesn't inspire you I don't know what will," said Mr. Dyer. And, taking up a handbill that lay upon his writing-table, he read aloud as follows:

"Five hundred pounds reward.—Missing, since Monday, September 20th, Irené, only daughter of Richard Golding, of Langford Hall, Langford Cross, Leicestershire. Age 18, height five feet seven; dark hair and eyes, olive complexion, small features; was dressed when she left home in dark blue serge walking costume, with white straw sailor hat trimmed with cream ribbon. Jewellery worn; plain gold brooch, leather strap bracelet holding small watch, and on the third finger of left hand a marquise ring consisting of one large diamond, surrounded with twelve rubies. Was last seen about ten o'clock on the morning of the 20th leaving Langford Hall Park for the high road leading to Langford Cross. The above reward will be paid to any one giving such information as will lead to the young lady's restoration to her home; or portions of the reward, according to the value of the information received. All communications to be addressed to the Chief Inspector, Police Station, Langford Cross."

"Was last seen on the 20th of September!" exclaimed Loveday, as Mr. Dyer finished reading. "Why, that is ten days ago! Do you mean to say that reward has not stimulated the energies of the local police and long ago put them on the traces of the missing girl?"

"It has stimulated their energies, not a doubt, for the local papers teem with accounts of the way in which the whole country about Langford has been turned upside down generally. Every river, far and near has been dragged; every wood scoured; every railway official at every station for miles round has been driven nearly mad with persistent cross-questioning. But all to no purpose. The affair remains as great a mystery as ever. The girl, as the handbill says, was seen leaving the Park for the high road by some children who chanced to be passing, but after that she seems to have disappeared as completely as if the earth had opened to receive her."

"Cannot her own people suggest any possible motive for her thus suddenly leaving home?"

"It appears not; they seem absolutely incapable of assigning any reason whatever for her extraordinary conduct. This morning I received a letter from Inspector Ramsay, asking me to get you to take up the case. Mr. Golding will not have the slightest objection to your staying at the Hall and thoroughly investigating the matter. Ramsay says it is just possible that they have concentrated too much attention on the search outside the house, and that a promising field for investigation may lie within."

"They should have thought of that before," said Loveday sharply. "I hope you declined the case. Here's the country inspector to the backbone! He'll keep a case in his own hands so long as there's a chance of success; then, when it becomes practically hopeless, hand it over to you just to keep his own failure in countenance by yours."

"Ye-es," said Mr. Dyer, slowly. "I suppose that's about it. But still, business has been slack of late—expenses are heavy—if you thought there was a ghost of a chance—"

"After ten days!" interrupted Miss Brooke, "when the house has settled down into routine, and every one has his story cut and dried, and all sorts of small details have been falsified or smudged over! Criminal cases are like fevers; they should be taken in hand within twenty-four hours."

"Yes, I know," said Mr. Dyer irritably, "but still, as I said before, business is slack—"

"Oh, well, if I'm to go, I'm to go, and there's an end of it," said Loveday resignedly. "I only say it would have been better, for the credit of the office, if you had declined such a hopeless affair. Tell me a little about this Mr. Richard Golding, who and what he is."

Mr. Dyer's temper grew serene again.

"He is a very wealthy man," he answered, "an Australian merchant; came over to England about a dozen years ago, and settled down at Langford Hall. He had, however, been living in Italy for some six or seven years previously. On his way home from Australia he did Italy, as so many Australians do, fell in love with a pretty girl, whom he met at Naples, and married her, and by her had this one child, Irené, who is causing such a sensation at the present moment."

"Is this Italian wife living?"

"No, she died just before Mr. Golding came to England. He has not yet married again, but I hear is on the point of so doing. The lady he contemplates making the second Mrs. Golding is a certain Mrs. Greenhow, a widow, who for the past year or so has acted as chaperon to his daughter and housekeeper to himself."

"It is possible that Miss Irené was not too well pleased at the idea of having a stepmother."

"Such is the fact. From all accounts she and her future stepmother did not get on at all well together. Miss Irené has a very hasty, imperious temper, and Mrs. Greenhow seems to have been quite incapable of holding her own with her. She was to have left the hall this month to make her preparations for the approaching wedding; the young lady's disappearance, however, has naturally brought matters to a standstill."

"Did Miss Golding take any money away with her, do you know?"

"Ah, nobody seems sure on that head. Mr. Golding gave her a liberal allowance and exacted no accounts. Sometimes she had her purse full at the end of the quarter, sometimes it was empty before her quarterly cheque had been cashed a week. I fear you will have to do without exact information on that most important point.

"She had lovers, of course?"

"Yes; in spite of her quick temper she seems to have been a lovable and most attractive young woman, with her half-Australian half-Italian parentage, and to have turned the heads of all the men in the neighbourhood. Only two, however, appear to have found the slightest favour in her eyes—a certain Lord Guilleroy, who owns nearly all the land for miles round Langford, and a young fellow called Gordon Cleeve, the only son of Sir Gordon Cleeve, a wealthy baronet. The girl seems to have coquetted pretty equally with these two; then suddenly, for some reason or other, she gives Mr. Cleeve to understand that his attentions are distasteful to her, and gives unequivocal encouragement to Lord Guilleroy. Gordon Cleeve does not sit down quietly under this treatment. He threatens to shoot first his rival, then himself, then Miss Golding; finally, does none of these three things, but starts off on a three years' journey round the world."

"Threatens to shoot her; starts off on a journey round the world," summed up Loveday. "Do you know the date of the day on which he left Langford?"

"Yes, it was on the 19th; the day before Miss Golding disappeared. But Ramsay has already traced him down to Brindisi; ascertained that he went on board the *Buckingham, en route* for Alexandria, and has beaten out the theory that he can, by any possibility, be connected with the affair. So I wouldn't advise you to look in that quarter for your clue."

"I am not at all sanguine about finding a clue in any quarter," said Loveday, as she rose to take leave.

She did not feel in the best of tempers, and was a little disposed to resent having a case, so to speak, forced upon her under such disadvantageous conditions.

Her last words to Mr. Dyer were almost the first she addressed to Inspector Ramsay when, towards the close of the day, she was met by him at Langford Cross Station. Ramsay was a lanky, bony Scotchman, sandy-haired and slow of speech.

"Our hopes centre on you; we trust you'll not disappoint us," he said, by way of a greeting.

His use of the plural number made Loveday turn in the direction of a tall, good-looking man, with a remarkably frank expression of countenance, who stood at the inspector's elbow.

"I am Lord Guilleroy," said this gentleman, coming forward. "Will you allow me to drive you to Langford Hall? My cab is waiting outside."

"Thank you; one moment," answered Loveday, again turning to Ramsay. "Now, do you wish," she said, addressing him, "to tell me anything beyond the facts you have already communicated to Mr. Dyer?"

"No-o," answered the inspector, slowly and sententiously. "I would rather not bias your mind in any direction by any theory of mine." ("It would be rather a waste of time to attempt such a thing," thought Loveday.) "The only additional fact I have to mention is one you would see for yourself so soon as you arrived at the Hall, namely, that Mr. Golding is keeping up with great difficulty—in fact, is on the verge of a break-down. He has not had half an hour's sleep since his daughter left home,—a serious thing that for a man at his age."

Loveday was favourably impressed with Lord Guilleroy. He gave her the idea of being a man of strong common-sense and great energy. His conversation was marked by a certain reserve. Although, however, he evidently declined to wear his heart upon his sleeve, it was easy to see, from a few words that escaped him, that if the search for Miss Golding proved fruitless his whole life would be wrecked.

He did not share Inspector Ramsay's wish not to bias Loveday's mind by any theory of his own.

"If I had a theory you should have it in a minute," he said, as he whipped up his horse and drove rapidly along the country road; "but I confess at the present moment my mind is a perfect blank on the matter. I have had a dozen theories, and have been compelled, one by one, to let them all go. I have suspected every one in turn, Cleeve, her own father (God forgive me!), her intended step-mother, the very servants in the house, and, one by one, circumstances have seemed to exonerate them all. It's bewildering—it's maddening! And most maddening of all it is to have to sit here with idle hands, when I would scour the earth from end to end to find her!"

The country around Langford Hall, like most of the hunting districts in Leicestershire, was as flat as if a gigantic stream-roller had passed over it. The Hall itself was a somewhat imposing Gothic structure, of rough grey stone. Very grey and drear it showed in the autumn landscape as Loveday drove in through the park gates and caught her first glimpse of it between the all but leafless elms that flanked the drive. The equinoctial gales had set in early this year, and heavy rains had helped forward their work of wreckage and destruction. The green sward of the park was near akin to a swamp; and the trout stream that flowed across it at an angle showed swollen to its very banks. The sky was leaden with gathering masses of clouds; a flight of rooks, wheeling low and flapping their black wings, with their mournful cawing, completed the dreariness of the scene.

"A companion picture, this," Loveday thought, "to the desolation that must reign within the house with the fate of its only daughter unknown—unguessed at even."

As she alighted at the hall door, a magnificent Newfoundland dog came bounding forth. Lord Guilleroy caressed it heartily.

"It was her dog," he explained. "We have tried in vain to make him track down his mistress—these dogs haven't the scent of hounds."

He excused himself from entering the house with Loveday.

"It's like a vault—a catacomb; I can't stand it," he said. "No, I'll take back my horse;" this was said to the man who stood waiting. "Tell Mr. Golding he'll see me round in the morning without fail."

Loveday was shown into the library, where Mr. Golding was waiting to receive her. In the circumstances no disguise as to her name and profession had been deemed necessary, and she was announced simply as Miss Brooke from Lynch Court.

Mr. Golding greeted her warmly. One glance at him convinced her that Inspector Ramsay had given no exaggerated account of the bereaved father. His face was wan and haggard; his head was bowed; his voice sounded strained and weak. He seemed incapable of speaking on any save the one topic that filled his thoughts.

"We pin our faith on you, Miss Brooke," he said; "you are our last hope. Now, tell me you do not despair of being able to end this awful suspense one way or another. A day or two more of it will put me into my coffin!"

"Miss Brooke will perhaps like to have some tea, and to rest a little, after her long journey before she begins to talk?" said a lady, at that moment entering the room and advancing towards her. Loveday could only conjecture that this was Mrs. Greenhow, for Mr. Golding was too preoccupied to make any attempt to an introduction.

Mrs. Greenhow was a small, slight woman, with fluffy hair and green-grey eyes. Her voice suggested a purr; her eyes, a scratch.

"Cat-tribe!" thought Loveday; "the velvet paw and the hidden claw— the exact antithesis, I should say, to one of Miss Golding's temperament."

Mr. Golding went back to the one subject he had at heart.

"You have had my daughter's photograph given to you, I've no doubt," he said; "but this I consider a far better likeness." Here he pointed to a portrait in pastels that hung above his writing-table. It was that of a large-eyed, handsome girl of eighteen, with a remarkably sweet expression about the mouth.

Mrs. Greenhow again interposed. "I think, if you don't mind my saying so," she said, "you would slightly mislead Miss Brooke if you led her to think that that was a perfect likeness of dear René. Much as I love the dear girl," here she turned to Loveday, "I'm bound to admit that one seldom or never saw her wearing such a sweet expression of countenance."

Mr. Golding frowned, and sharply changed the subject.

"Tell me, Miss Brooke," he said, "what was your first impression when the facts of the case were submitted to you? I have been told that first impressions with you are generally infallible."

Loveday parried the question.

"I am not at present sure that I am in possession of all the facts," she answered. "There are one or two questions I particularly want to ask— you must forgive me if they seem to you a little irrelevant to the matter in hand. First and foremost, I want to know if any formal good-bye took place between your daughter and Mr. Gordon Cleeve?"

"I think not. A sudden coolness arose between them, and the young fellow went away without so much as shaking hands with me."

"I fear an irreparable breach has occurred between the Cleeves and yourself on account of dear René's extraordinary treatment of Gordon," said Mrs. Greenhow sweetly.

"There was no extraordinary treatment," said Mr. Golding, now almost in anger. "My daughter and Mr. Cleeve were good friends—nothing more, I assure you—until one day René saw him cruelly thrashing one of his setters, and after that she cut him dead—would have nothing whatever to do with him."

"Maddalena told Inspector Ramsay," said Mrs. Greenhow, sweetly still, "that on the evening before Gordon Cleeve left Langford dear René received a note from him—"

"Which she tossed unopened into the fire," finished Mr. Golding.

"Who is Maddalena?" interrupted Loveday.

"My daughter's maid. I brought her over from Naples twelve years ago as nurse, and as René grew older she naturally enough fell into her duties as René's maid. She is a dear, faithful creature; her aunt was nurse to René's mother."

"Is it possible for Maddalena to be told off to wait upon me while I am in the house?" asked Loveday, turning to Mrs. Greenhow.

"Certainly, if you wish it. At the same time, I warn you that she is not in a particularly amiable frame of mind just now, and will be very likely to be sullen and disobliging," answered the lady.

"Maddalena is not generally either one or the other," said Mr. Golding deprecatingly; "but just now she is a little unlike herself. The truth is, all the servants have been a little too rigorously cross-examined by the police on matters of which they could have absolutely no knowledge, and Ramsay made such a dead set at Lena that the girl felt herself insulted, grew sullen, and refused to open her lips."

"She must be handled judiciously. I suppose she was broken-hearted when Miss Golding did not return from her morning's walk?"

A reply was prevented by the entrance of a servant with a telegram in his hand.

Mr. Golding tore it open, and, in a trembling voice, read aloud as follows:

"Some one answering to the description of your daughter was seen yesterday in the Champs Elysées, but disappeared before she could be detained. Watch arrivals at Folkestone and Dover."

The telegram was dated from Paris, and was from M. Dulau, of the Paris police. Mr. Golding's agitation was pitiable.

"Great heavens! is it possible?" he cried, putting his hand to his forehead as if stunned. "I'll start for Dover—no, Paris, I think, at once." He staggered to his feet, looking around him in a dazed and bewildered fashion. He might as well have talked of starting for the moon or the north star.

CATHERINE LOUISA PIRKIS

"Pardon me," said Loveday, "Inspector Ramsay is the right person to deal with that telegram. It should be sent to him at once."

Mr. Golding sank back in his chair, trembling from head to foot.

"I think you are right," he said faintly. "I might break down and lose a possible chance."

Then he turned once more to the man, who stood waiting for orders, and desired him to take the fastest horse to the stables and ride at once with the telegram to the Inspector.

"And," he added, "on your way back call at the Castle, see Lord Guilleroy, and give him the news." He turned a pleading face towards Loveday. "This is good news—you consider it good news, do you not?" he asked piteously.

"It won't do to depend too much on it, will it?" said Mrs. Greenhow. "You see, there have been so many false alarms—if I may use the word."—This was said to Loveday.—"Three times last week we had telegrams from different parts of the country saying dear René had been seen—now here, now there, I think there must be a good many girls like her wandering about the world."

"The dress has something to do with it, no doubt," answered Loveday; "it is not a very distinctive one. Still, we must hope for the best. It is possible, of course, that at this very moment the young lady may be on her way home with a full explanation of what has seemed extraordinary conduct on her part. Now, if you will allow me, I will go to my room. And will you please give the order that Maddalena shall follow me there as quickly as possible?"

Loveday's thoughts were very busy when, in the quietude of her own room, she sank into an easy chair beside the fire. The case to which she had so unwillingly devoted her attention was beginning to present some interesting intricacies. She passed in view the *dramatis personae* of the little drama which she could only hope might not end in a tragedy. The broken-hearted father; the would-be-step-mother, with her feline affinities; the faithful maid; the cruel-tempered lover; the open-faced, energetic one; each in turn received their meed of attention.

"That man would be one to depend on in an emergency," she said to herself, allowing her thoughts to dwell a little longer upon Lord Guilleroy than upon the others. "He has, I should say, a good head on his shoulders and—"

But here a tap-tap at the door brought her thinking to a standstill, and in response to her "come in" the door opened and the maid Lena entered.

She was a tall, black-eyed, dark-skinned woman of about thirty, dressed in a neat black stuff gown. Twelve years of English domestic life had considerably modified the outer tokens of her nationality; a gold dagger that kept a thick coil of hair in its place, and a massive Roman-cut cameo ring on the third finger of her right hand, were about the only things that differentiated her appearance from that of the ordinary English lady's maid. Possibly as a rule she wore a pleasant, smiling expression of countenance. For the moment, however, her face was shadowed by a sullen scowl, that said plainly as words could: "I am here very much against my will, and intend to render you the most unwilling of services."

Loveday felt that she must be taken in hand at once.

"You are Miss Golding's maid, I believe?" she said in a short, sharp tone.

"Yes, madame." This in a slow, sullen one.

"Very well, Kindly unstrap that portmanteau and open my dressing-bag. I am glad you are to wait upon me while I am here. I don't suppose you ever before in your life acted maid to a lady detective?"

"Never, madame." This in a still more sullen tone than before.

"Ah, it will be a new experience to you, and I hope that it may be made a profitable one also. Tell me, are you saving up money to get married?"

Lena, on her knees unstrapping the portmanteau, started and looked up.

"How does madame know that?" she asked, Loveday pointed to the cameo ring on her third finger. "I only guessed at such a possibility," she answered. "Well, now, Lena, I am going to make you an offer. I will give you fifty pounds—fifty, remember, in English gold—if you will procure for me certain information that I require in the prosecution of my work here."

The sullen look on Lena's face deepened.

"I am a servant of the house," she answered, bending lower over the portmanteau; "I do not sell its secrets even for English gold."

"But it is not the secrets of your master's house I am wanting to buy—no, nor anybody else's secrets; I only want you to procure for me certain information that I could easily have procured for myself if I had been a little sooner on the scene. And the information I want relates to no one inside the house, but some one outside of it—Mr. Gordon Cleeve."

The sullen look on Lena's face gave place to one of intense, unutterable relief.

"Mr. Gordon Cleeve!" she repeated. "Oh-h, for fifty pounds, I will undertake to bring madame a good deal of information about him; I know some of the servants in Sir Gordon's house. I know, too, the mother of Mr. Cleeve's valet who has started with him on his journey round the world."

"Good. So, then, it is a bargain. Now, Lena, tell me truly, is this Mr. Cleeve a great favourite with you?"

"With me! Ah, the good God forbid, madame! I never liked him; I used to say to Miss René when I brought her his flowers and his notes: 'Have nothing to do with him, he is cruel—bad at heart.'"

"Ah, yes; I read all that in your face when I mentioned his name. Now what I want you first and foremost to do for me is to find out how this young man spent the last day that he was at Langford. I want you to bring me a report of his doings—as exact a report as possible—on the 18th of this month."

"I will do my best, madame."

"Very good. Now, there is something else. Would you be greatly surprised if I told you that the young man did not sail in the *Buckingham* from Brindisi as is generally supposed?"

"Madame! Inspector Ramsay said he had ascertained beyond a doubt that Mr. Cleeve went on board the *Buckingham* at Brindisi!"

"Ah, to go on board is one thing; to sail is another! Now, listen, Lena, very carefully to what I am going to say. I am expecting daily to receive some most important information respecting this gentleman's movements, and I may want some one to set off at a minute's notice for Paris, perhaps; or, perhaps, Florence or Naples, to verify that information: would you do this for me?—of course, I would supply you with money and full details as to your journey."

A flush of pleasure passed over Lena's face.

"Yes, madame," she answered; "if you could get my master's permission for me to go."

"I will undertake to do so." She pondered a moment, then added a little tentatively, and closely watching Lena's face as she asked the question, "I suppose Miss Golding resembled her mother in appearance—I do not see any likeness between her portrait and her father."

Lena's sullenness and stateliness had vanished together now, and once upon the topic of her nursling she was the warm-hearted, enthusiastic

Italian woman once more. She became voluble in her description of her dear Miss René, her beauty, her fascinating ways, which she traced entirely to the Italian blood that flowed in her veins; and anecdote after anecdote she related of the happy time when they lived among the lakes and mountains of her native land.

The room grew dark and darker, while she gossiped apace, and presently the dressing-bell clanged through the house.

"Light the candles now," said Loveday, rising from her seat beside the fire; "draw down the blinds and shut out that dreary autumn scene, it sets me shivering!"

It might well do so. The black clouds had fulfilled their threat, and rain was now dashing in torrents against the panes. A tall sycamore, immediately outside the window, creaked and groaned dismally in response to the wind that came whistling round the corner of the house, and between the swaying and all but leafless elms Loveday could catch a glimpse of the grey, winding trout stream, swollen now to its limits and threatening to overflow its banks.

Dinner that night was in keeping with the gloom that overhung the house within and without; although the telegram from Paris had seemed to let in a ray of hope, Mr. Golding was evidently afraid to put much trust in it.

"As Mrs. Greenhow says, 'we have had so many disappointments,'" he said sadly, as he took his place at table. "So many false clues—false scents started. Ramsay has at once put himself in communication with the police at Boulogne and Calais, as well as at Dover and Folkestone. We can only pray that something may come of it!"

"And dear Lord Guilleroy," chimed in Mrs. Greenhow, in her soft, purring voice, "has started for Paris immediately. The young man has such a vast amount of energy, and thinks he can do the work of the police better than they can do it for themselves."

"That's hardly a fair way of putting it, Clare," interrupted Mr. Golding irritably; "he is working heart and soul with the police, and thinks it advisable that some one representing me should be in Paris, in case an emergency should arise; also he wants himself to question Dulau respecting my daughter's sudden appearance and disappearance in the Paris streets. Guilleroy," here he turned to Loveday, "is devotedly attached to my daughter, and—why, Dryad, what's the matter, old man? down, down! Don't growl and whine in that miserable fashion."

He had broken off to address these words to the Newfoundland, who, until that moment, had been comfortably stretched on the hearth-rug before the fire, but who now had suddenly started to his feet with ears erect, and given a prolonged growl, that ended in something akin to a whine.

"It may be a fox trotting past the window," said Mrs. Greenhow, whipping at the dog with her lace handkerchief. But Dryad was not to be so easily subdued. With his nose to the ground now he was sniffing uneasily at and around the heavy curtains that half draped the long French windows of the room.

"Something has evidently disturbed him. Why not let him out into the garden?" said Loveday. And Mr. Golding, with a "Hey, Dryad, go find!" unfastened the window and let the dog out into the windy darkness.

Dinner was a short meal that night. It was easy to see that it was only by a strong effort of will that Mr. Golding kept his place at table, and made even a pretence of eating.

At the close of the meal Loveday asked for a quiet corner, in which to write some business letters, and was shown into the library by Mr. Golding.

"You'll find all you require here, I think," he said, with something of a sigh, as he placed a chair for her at a lady's davenport. "This was René's favourite corner, and here are the last flowers she gathered—dead, all dead, but I will not have them touched!" He broke off abruptly, set down the vase of dead asters which he had taken in his hand, and quitted the room, leaving Loveday to the use of René's pen, ink, paper, and blotting-pad.

Loveday soon became absorbed in her business letters. Time flew swiftly, and it was not until a clock on the mantelpiece chimed the hour—ten o'clock—that she gave a thought as to what might be the hour for retiring at the Hall.

Something else beside the striking of the clock almost simultaneously caught her ear—the whining and scratching of a dog at one of the windows. These, like those of the dining-room, opened as doors into an outside verandah. They were, however, closely shuttered, and Loveday had to ring for a servant to undo the patent fastener.

So soon as the window was opened Dryad rushed into the room, plastered with mud, and dripping with water from every hair.

"He must have been in the stream," said the footman, trying to collar the dog and lead him out of the room.

"Stop! one moment!" cried Loveday, for her eye had caught sight of something hanging in shreds between the dog's teeth. She bent over him, patting and soothing him, and contrived to disentangle those shreds, which a closer examination proved to be a few tattered fragments of dark blue serge.

"Is your letter-writing nearly ended, Miss Brooke?" asked Mr. Golding, at that moment entering the room.

For reply, Loveday held up the shreds of blue serge. His face grew ashen white; he needed no explanation; those shreds and the dripping dog seemed to tell their own tale.

"Great heavens!" he cried, "why did I not follow the dog out! There must be a search at once. Get men, lanterns, ropes, a ladder—the dog, too, will be of use."

A terrible energy took possession of him. "Find, Dryad, find!" he shouted to the dog, and then, hatless and thin-shoed as he was, he rushed out into the darkness with Dryad at his heels.

In less than five minutes afterwards the whole of the men-servants of the house, with lanterns, ropes, and a ladder long enough to span the stream, had followed him. The wind had fallen, the rain had ceased now, and a watery half-moon was struggling through the thin, flying clouds. Loveday and Mrs. Greenhow, standing beneath the verandah, watched the men disappear in the direction of the trout stream, whither Dryad had led the way. From time to time shouts came to them, through the night stillness, of "This way!" "No, here!" together with Dryad's sharp bark and the occasional distant flash of a bull's-eye lantern. It was not until nearly half an hour afterwards that one of the men came running back to the house with a solemn white face and a pitiful tale. He wanted something that would serve for a stretcher, he said in a subdued tone— the two-fold oak screen in the hall would do—and please, into which room was "it" to be brought?—

On the following evening Mr. Dyer received a lengthy dispatch from Miss Brooke, which ran as follows:—

LANGFORD HALL

"This is to supplement my telegram of an hour back, telling you of the finding of Miss Golding's body in the stream that runs through her father's grounds. Mr. Golding has himself identified the body, and has now utterly collapsed. At the present moment it seems rather doubtful whether he will be

CATHERINE LOUISA PIRKIS

in a fit state to give evidence at the inquest, which will be held to-morrow. Miss Golding appears to be dressed as she was when she left home, with this notable exception—the marquise ring has disappeared from the third finger of her left hand, and in its stead she wears a plain gold wedding-ring. Now this is a remarkable circumstance, and strikes a strange keynote to my mind. I am writing hurriedly, and can only give you the most important points in this very singular case. The maid, Lena, a reserved, self-contained woman, gave way to a passion of grief when the young lady's body was brought in and laid upon her own bed. She insisted on performing all the last sad offices for the dead, however, in spite of her grief, and is now, I am glad to say, calmer and capable of a little quiet conversation with me. I keep her continually in attendance on me, as I am rather anxious to keep my eye on her just now. I have telegraphed to Lord Guilleroy, asking him, in spite of the terrible news which will in due course reach him, to be good enough to remain in Paris awaiting directions from me, which may have to be carried out at a minute's notice. I hope to have further news to send a little later on."

Mr. Dyer laid aside the letter with a grunt of dissatisfaction.

"Well," he said to himself, "I suppose she expects me to be able to read between the lines, but I'm bothered if I can make head or tail of it all. She seems to me to be going a little wide of the mark just now; it might be as well to give her a hint." So he dashed off a few brief lines as follows:—

"I suppose you are concentrating now on finding out what were Miss Golding's movements while absent from her home. It seems to me this could be better done in Paris than at Langford Hall. The ring on her finger necessarily implies that she has gone through a marriage service somewhere, and as she was seen in Paris a day or two ago, it is as likely as not that the ceremony took place there. The Paris police could give you 'yea or nay' on this matter within twenty-four hours. As to the maid, Lena, I think you are laying too much stress upon her possible knowledge of her mistress's movements.

"If she had been tied down to secrecy by promise of reward, she would naturally, now that all such promises are rendered futile, reveal all she knows on the matter—she has nothing to gain by keeping the secrets of the dead."

This letter crossed on its road a telegram from Loveday running thus:—

"Inquest over. Verdict, 'Found drowned, but how deceased got into the water there is no evidence to show.' Funeral takes place to-morrow; Mr. Golding delirious with brain fever."

On the day following Mr. Dyer received a second letter from Loveday. Thus it ran:—

"The funeral is over; Mr. Golding is much worse, I have dispatched Lena to Paris, telling her I require her services there to follow up a clue I hold respecting Mr. Gordon Cleeve, and promising her rewards commensurate with the manner in which she carries out my orders. I have also written to Lord Guilleroy, telling him the sort of assistance I require from him. If he is the man I take him for he will be more useful to me than all the Paris police put together. I will answer your letter in detail in a day or two. The neighbourhood is still in a state of great excitement, and all sorts of wild reports are flying about. Ramsay and Dulau have traced a lady, dressed in dark blue serge, and answering in other respects to Miss Golding's description, from the Gare du Midi, Paris, step by step to her arrival at Langford Cross, whence, poor thing, she must have walked through the pouring rain to the Hall. I do not see, however, that this information helps us forward one step towards the solution of the mystery of the girl's disappearance. Ramsay is a little inclined to criticize what he calls my 'leisurely handling' of the case. Mrs. Greenhow, who is a terribly empty-headed, but at the same time essentially hard-natured little woman, appears disposed to follow suit, and has more than once thrown out hints that my stay in the house is being unnecessarily prolonged. As there is practically no further necessity for my remaining at the Hall, I have told her that I shall to-day take up my quarters at the Roebuck Inn (by courtesy hotel), at Langford Cross. I believe she is unfeignedly glad at what she considers the ending of the affair. The imperious yet fascinating young lady no doubt ruled her and the household generally with a rod of iron, and the little woman, I feel sure, if she had dared, would have ordered bonfires and a general rejoicing on the day of the funeral. Well, I have not much sympathy with her, and am preparing for her a shock to her not too-sensitive nerves which she little suspects. My chief anxiety at the present moment is Mr. Golding, who still remains unconscious. I have requested the doctors to send me two bulletins daily of his condition, which I fear is a most serious one."

There could be little doubt on this head. The doctors' verdict on the day that Loveday left Langford Hall for "The Roebuck" was: "Absolutely no hope." The bulletin brought to her on the following morning was "Condition remains unchanged." On the third day, however, the report was "Slight improvement." Then followed the welcome bulletins of "Improvement maintained," and "Out of danger," to be followed by the most welcome report of all: "Is making steady progress towards recovery."

"It is Mr. Golding's illness that has kept me here so long," said Loveday to Inspector Ramsay, as if by way of apology for her continued presence on the scene. "I think, however, I can see my way to departure now. Going to Paris? Oh, dear me, no. I have telegraphed to Mr. Dyer to expect me back the day after to-morrow; if you will like to come to me here, or will meet me at Langford Cross Station, I will give you a full report of all I have done since I took the case in hand. Now I am going to the Hall to ascertain at what hour to-morrow it will be convenient for me to say good-bye to Mr. Golding."

More than this Ramsay was unable to extract from Miss Brooke. His open strictures upon what he called her "leisurely handling of the case" had put her upon her mettle, and she had decided that Ramsay and his colleagues should be taught that Lynch Court had a special way of doing things, and could hold its own with the best.

On her way to the Hall Loveday called at the post-office, and there had a letter with a London postmark handed to her. This she at once opened and read, and then dispatched a reply to it by telegram. The reply was an enigmatic one to the village post-master, for Loveday, after a few casual questions as to his knowledge of Continental languages, chose German as her medium of communication. The address, however, "to Lord Guilleroy, at Charing Cross Hotel," was plain reading enough.

At the Hall Loveday found Mrs. Greenhow in an active state of mind. Mr. Golding, she informed her with a sweet effusiveness, would come downstairs for a short time on the following day, and she was doing all that lay in her power to put out of sight anything that might awaken painful recollections. "I have had dear René's harp removed to a lumber room, her portrait taken down from the library wall," she said, in her usual purring tones; "and her davenport is being wheeled into my own sitting-room. Poor dear René! If only she could have been taught to govern her willful temper a happier fate might have befallen her. What that fate was I suppose we shall never know now."

Loveday's only reply to this was to ask for an exact report of the doctor's opinion of Mr. Golding's condition. Mrs. Greenhow put her handkerchief to her eyes as she answered that Doctor Godwin's opinion was that, so far as bodily strength was concerned, he was considerably better, but that his mental condition was a serious one. His brain appeared to be in a state of semi-stupefaction, which it was possible might be indicative of the softening of its tissues.

Loveday expressed a wish to see this doctor—to time her farewell visit to Mr. Golding on the following day with Dr. Godwin's daily call. In fact, she would like a little private talk with him before she went in to see his patient.

To all this Mrs. Greenhow offered no objection. Lady detectives, she said to herself, were a race apart, and had a curious way of doing things; but, thank Heaven, she would soon see the last of this one!

THE STORMY AUTUMNAL WEATHER HAD given place now to a brief spell of late summer sunshine, and on the last day of her visit to Langford, Miss Brooke had a cheerier view of the Hall and its surroundings than she had had on the day of her arrival there. The trout stream had retreated to its natural proportions, and showed like a streak of molten silver—not a grey, turbid flood—in the bright sunlight that played at hide-and-seek between the branches of the stript elms. Even the old rooks seemed to have a cheery undernote to their "caw, caw" as they wheeled about the old house; and Dryad himself, as he once more came bounding forth to greet her, appeared to her fancy to have a less dolorous ring in his noisy bark.

"That dog is a perfect nuisance—has been utterly spoilt. I must have him chained up," said Mrs. Greenhow, as she led the way into a room where Dr. Godwin sat awaiting Loveday. She introduced them one to the other. "Shall I remain, or do you wish to converse alone?" she asked.

And as Loveday answered with decision "Alone," the little woman had no choice but to withdraw, wondering once more over the vagaries of lady detectives.

Half an hour afterwards the doctor, a clever-looking, active little man, led the way into the library where Mr. Golding was seated.

Loveday was greatly shocked at the change which a few days' illness had wrought in him. His chair was drawn close to the window, and the autumn sunshine that filled the room threw into pitiful relief his shrunken frame and pallid face, aged now by about a dozen years. His eyes were closed, his head was bent low on his breast, and he did not lift it as the door opened.

"You need not remain," said Dr. Godwin to the nurse, who rose as they entered; and Loveday and the doctor were left alone with the patient.

Loveday drew near softly. "I am going back to town this evening, and have come to say good-bye," she said, extending her hand.

Mr. Golding opened his eyes, staring vaguely at the extended hand. "To say good-bye!" he repeated, in a dreamy, far-away tone.

"I am Miss Brooke," Loveday explained. "I came down from London to investigate the strange circumstances connected with your daughter's disappearance."

"My daughter's disappearance!" He started and began to tremble violently.

The doctor had his hand on his patient's pulse now.

"I have conducted my investigations under somewhat disadvantageous circumstances," Loveday went on quietly, "and, for a time, with but little result. A few days back, however, I received important information from Lord Guilleroy, and to-day I have seen and communicated with him. In fact, it was his carriage that brought me to your house this afternoon."

"Lord Guilleroy!" repeated Mr. Golding slowly. His voice had a more natural ring in it; recollection, although, perhaps, a painful one, seemed to sound in it.

"Yes. He said he would wander about the park until I had seen and prepared you for his visit. Ah! there he is coming up the drive."

Here she drew back the curtain that half draped the open window.

This window commanded a good view of the drive, with its overarching elms, that led from the lodge gates to the house. Along that drive two persons were advancing at that moment in leisurely fashion; one of those two was undoubtedly Lord Guilleroy, the other was a tall, graceful girl, dressed in deep mourning.

Mr. Golding's eyes followed Loveday's at first with a blank, expressionless stare. Then, little by little, that stare changed into a look of intelligence and recognition. His face grew ashen white, then a wave of colour swept over it.

"Lord Guilleroy, yes," he said, panting and struggling for breath. "But—but who is that walking with him? Tell me, tell me quickly, for the love of Heaven!"

He tried to rise to his feet, but his limbs failed him. The doctor poured out a cordial, and put it to his lips.

"Drink this, please," he said. "Now tell him quickly," he whispered to Loveday.

"That young lady," she resumed calmly, "is your daughter René. She drove up with me and Lord Guilleroy from Langford Cross. Shall I ask her to come in and see you? She is only waiting for Dr. Godwin's permission to do so."

Time to grant or refuse that permission, however, was not accorded to Dr. Godwin. René—a sadder, sweeter-faced René than the one who had so impetuously discarded home and father—now stood outside in the "half-sun, half-shade" of the verandah, and had caught the sound of Loveday's last words.

She swept impetuously past her into the room.

"Father, father!" she said, as she knelt down beside his chair, "I have come back at last! Are you not glad to see me?"

"I DARESAY IT ALL SEEMS very mysterious to you," said Loveday to Inspector Ramsay, as together they paced the platform of Langford Cross Station, waiting for the incoming of the London train, "but, I assure you, it all admits of the easiest and simplest of explanations— Who on earth was it that the inquest was held over, and who was buried about a week ago, do you say? Oh, that was Mr. Golding's wife, Irené, daughter of Count Mascagni, of Alguida, in South Italy, whom every one believed to be dead. It is her history that holds the key to the whole affair from first to last. I will begin at the beginning, and tell you her

CATHERINE LOUISA PIRKIS

story as nearly as possible as it was told to me. To be quite frank with you, I would have admitted you long ago into my confidence, and told you, step by step, how things were working themselves out, if you had not offended me by criticizing my method of doing my work."

"I'm sure I'm very sorry," here broke in Ramsay in a deprecating tone.

"Oh, pray don't mention it. Let me see, where was I? Ah, I must go back some nineteen or twenty years in Mr. Golding's life in order to make things clear to you. The particulars which I had from Mr. Dyer, and which I fancy you supplied him with, respecting Mr. Golding's early life were so meager that directly I arrived at the Hall I set to work to supplement them; this I contrived to do in a before-dinner chat with Lena, Miss Golding's maid. I found out through her that Irené Mascagni was a typical Italian woman of the half-educated, passionate, beautiful, animal kind, and that Mr. Golding's early married life was anything but a happy one. Irené was motherless, and had been so spoilt from babyhood upwards by her old nurse, Lena's aunt, that she could not brook the slightest opposition to her whims and wishes. She was a great coquette also; lovers were an absolute necessity to her. Remonstrance on Mr. Golding's part was useless; Irené met it by appeals to her father for protection against what she considered her husband's brutality; in consequence, a serious quarrel ensued between the Count and Mr. Golding, and when the latter announced his intention of breaking up his Italian home and buying an estate in England, Irené, accompanied by her nurse, Antonia, left her husband and little daughter and went back to her father's house, vowing that nothing would induce her to leave her beloved Italy. At this crisis in his affairs, Mr. Golding was suddenly compelled to undertake a journey to Australia to adjust certain complicated matters of business. He took with him on this voyage his little girl, René, and her nurse—now her maid, Lena. The visit to Australia in all occupied about six months. During that time no communication of any sort passed between him and his wife or her father. He resolved, however, to make one more effort to induce Irené to return to her home and her duty; and, with this object, he went to Naples on his return to Europe and wrote to his wife from there, asking her to appoint a day for a meeting. In reply to this letter he received a visit from Antonia, who, with a great show of sorrow, informed him that Irené had caught a fever during his absence, and had died, and now lay buried in the family vault at Alguida. Mr. Golding's grief at the tidings was no doubt mitigated by the recollection of the unfortunate married life he had led. He made no attempt to communicate with Count Mascagni, started at once for England, and set up his establishment at Langford Hall. All this, with the exception of the name of Irené's father and that of his estate, was told me by Lena, who, I may mention in passing, laid great stress upon the wonderful likeness that existed between Miss Golding and her mother. She was, she said, the exact counterpart of what her mother had been at her age."

"It is marvelous to me how you contrived to get anything out of that woman Lena," said Ramsay; "she was most obstinately taciturn with me."

"Pardon me if I say that was because she had been most injudiciously handled. In the circumstances it would never have occurred to me to put a single direct question to her, although I like you, felt convinced that she was the one and only person likely to be in her young mistress's confidence. So fully imbued was I with this idea that I felt certain that, if she could be sent out of the house on any pretext, by closely following her movements we should, sooner or later, come upon the traces of Miss Golding. To attain this end, I feigned suspicion of Mr. Gordon Cleeve, and promised her rewards if she would bring me tidings of his doings. This was to pave the way to dismissing her on a journey to Italy. It also had the most welcome effect of calming her mind and convincing her of my belief in her innocence. With her fears thus allayed, I found her no longer sullen but communicative to a degree."

"Pardon my interrupting you at this point, but will you kindly tell me what, in the first instance, aroused your suspicious as to the identity of the person 'found drowned' by the coroner's jury?"

"Lena's conduct when the body was brought into the house. I should, however, tell you that a keynote of suspicion as to the possibility of Mrs. Golding being still alive had been struck when, as I sat writing at Miss Golding's davenport, I found the words "Mia Madre" scribbled here and there on her blotting-pad. Now what, I said to myself, could, after all these years, have turned her thoughts to her mother and her early Italian home? The wedding-ring on the lady's finger, coupled with Lena's statement as to Miss Golding's marvelous likeness to her mother, together with an exclamation of Mr. Golding's, after identifying the body, that his daughter had 'aged by a dozen years,' made these suspicions grow stronger. It was, however, Lena's own conduct that resolved them into positive certainty. I watched her narrowly after the body had been brought into the house. At first her grief was passionate and intense, and in it she let fall—in Italian—the extraordinary exclamation that a woman should break her heart for her lover, not for her mother. Then she, too, went into the room where the body lay—went in weeping, came out dry-eyed, and in the most methodical manner set to work to perform the last sad offices for the dead."

"Ah, yes, I see. Pray go on."

"It was on the day of the funeral, if you remember, that I dispatched Lena to Paris. I had previously written to Lord Guilleroy, hinting my suspicions, and begging him, in spite of everything, to remain at Paris, and to carry out any directions I might send him to the very letter. On dispatching Lena, I again wrote to him, telling him when she would arrive, where she would put up, and bidding him keep his eye on her, and follow her movements step by step. From Paris, I sent Lena on to Naples, bidding her await further orders there, and, all unknown to her, the train that carried her thither, carried also Lord Guilleroy. Naples had been the only place she had mentioned to me by name in her gossip about her life in Italy, but I felt confident, from some casual remarks she had let fall, that Irené Mascagni's early home, as well, also, as the home of her own lover, was within easy reach of the city. It was only natural to conjecture that if I kept her waiting there for orders she would utilize the opportunity for paying a visit to her friends and relatives, and also to her young mistress, if she were, as I supposed, in that neighbourhood. The result proved my conjecture correct."

"And Lord Guilleroy, thus following her movements, step by step, came upon her and Miss Golding in company?"

"He did. I think Lord Guilleroy deserves high encomium for the way in which he performed his share in this somewhat intricate case. No trained detective could have done better. He tracked Lena home to Alguida, a small hamlet within fifteen miles of Naples, and came upon her talking to Miss Golding, who stood at the gate of her grandfather's chateau dressed in her mother's Neapolitan dress. Miss Golding was unfeignedly glad to be taken possession of, so to speak, by one of her father's English friends, for she was becoming nervous and distressed at the position in which she found herself. Her mother was dead; her grandfather, a man of a violent temper, refused to allow her to leave his chateau, as he alleged he required, in his old age, the attendance of one who was his own kith and kin. Also there was in her mind a natural shrinking from the story she would have to tell her father, and the fear lest he might not be willing to forgive her for the part she had played. Nothing could have been more opportune than Lord Guilleroy's arrival. Miss Golding accorded to him her full confidence, and from this point the story ceases to be mine and becomes Lord Guilleroy's as communicated to him by Miss Golding."

"It is, in fact, the other half of the story that was told you by Lena?"

"It is; it starts from the period, twelve years back, when Mrs. Golding was supposed by her husband and child to be dead. Instead of dying, however, she had, after a month's stay at her father's lonely country house, joined a company of actors, then passing through Alguida. Her great personal beauty ensured her ready admission to the corps; and in her new life, no doubt, her vanity and innate love of coquetry found ample gratification. The faithful old nurse had followed her in her new career; the dramatic corps was actually in Naples when Mr. Golding arrived there, and the two women, neither of whom was disposed to enter upon the dull routine of English domestic life, had fabricated the lie in order the more effectually to retain their liberty. It is most probable that Count Mascagni knew nothing whatever of his daughter's movements at this period of her career. It is possible that, after a time, he may have believed her to be dead, for eleven years passed without his receiving any communication from her."

"Eleven years! Was she on the stage the whole of that time?"

"I have not been able to ascertain—in fact, I have not been very keen in making inquiries on this point, for it really is of little or no importance to the case. So far as we are concerned, her career is of importance only after her return to her father's house, now about a year ago. She came back one day, attended by Antonia, evidently out of health and in great poverty. Her father received her back conditionally; she had disgraced him and his ancient name, he said; dead she was supposed to be by her friends, dead she must remain—she must go nowhere, she must see no one."

"Ah, a sad story! And I suppose after a time the poor woman's thoughts flew to her husband and little daughter?"

"Yes. Antonia wrote to Lena that the mother was dying for the sight of her child, and implored her to tell René that her mother lived—a mother who had been cruelly treated alike by husband and father—and beg her, at all hazards, to come to her, that she might clasp her in her arms before the shadows of death closed in around her. This part of the story I had from René herself as we drove together to the Hall. The girl told me that when she read that letter all her blood was stirred within her. She was seized with a burning desire there and then to kiss that mother and to right her wrongs. For the moment she hated her father, felt that she must at once confront him and denounce him for his cruelty. Second thoughts suggested another course. Her father might forbid her all intercourse with her mother; she had plenty of money, why not start for Italy at once, and from her mother's lips dictate to her father the terms on which she would return to her English home? So the journey was planned, and Lena was promised by the young lady a pair of her handsome diamond earrings if she kept her secret till she herself gave her permission to speak. Not so much as a hand-bag was packed, for fear of exciting attention in the house; the undistinctive blue serge and sailor hat—supplemented subsequently by a thick veil—were selected as a travelling dress. Market-day at Langford, with a crowded railway station, was chosen for the day of departure, and the young lady walked the two miles that lay between it and her father's house in easy, leisurely fashion, as if she contemplated nothing more serious than a morning walk."

"Of course, so soon as she reached London all was plain sailing to her?"

"Yes. Lena, no doubt, supplied her with all necessary details respecting her journey. When she arrived at the Chateau Mascagni, she appears to have at once thoroughly succumbed to her mother's influence. Out of health although that mother was, René described her to me as the most fascinating woman she had ever met. I suppose the likeness between the two must have been something remarkable, for René said, after she had been a few days in the house and the mother had rallied a little in strength, the servants declared it was only by their dress that they could distinguish one from the other. On the fourth day after Miss Golding's arrival at the Chateau, her mother met her with a plan which, for fear of the effect that a refusal might have upon her health, she at once fell in with. It was to the effect that, instead of attempting negotiations with Mr. Golding through lawyers or by letter, she should herself go to him at his country house, throw herself upon his generosity, plead for forgiveness, and beg to be taken back to his heart once more."

"But why did not Miss René accompany her mother on this journey?"

"René was a force to be held in reserve. If her father refused her mother's request, she in her turn would refuse to return to her home, but would live on with her mother and grandfather at Alguida. The girl appears to have entertained bitter feelings against her father at this juncture—feelings possibly intensified by the thought of the sort of step-mother he intended to bestow upon her."

"Well, anyhow, so far as I can make out, Miss René's own mother hadn't much to boast of—in the way of common sense, at any rate. In fact, the two together appear to me to have acted more like a couple of school-girls than anything else. What made Mrs. Golding dress up in her daughter's clothes?"

"That, I believe, was a matter of convenience merely. Mrs. Golding had no money, and her father was not over-burdened with riches, and what little he had he held tightly. She had, for some reason or other, returned home with next to no wardrobe; René's dress was suitable for travelling, and not likely to attract attention. They neither of them seem to have given a thought to the possibility of rewards being offered for tidings of René; and thus, no doubt, while waiting for her train in Paris, Mrs. Golding did not hesitate to show herself in Paris streets. I need not go into the details of her journey to Langford; they are already known to you. The poor woman, not seeing any conveyance at the country station, must have walked in the drenching rain to the Hall. At the hall door, possibly, her courage suddenly failed her, and, instead of ringing for admission, she creeps to a window to get a glimpse of the home-life within. That glimpse is fatal. She sees her husband and the woman he intends to marry seated together at table. She takes in at a glance the refinement of the home, together with the rigid conventionality of English domestic life. A wave of memory, perhaps, brings before her episodes in her past career altogether out of tune with this home picture. She feels the impracticability of the mission on which she is bent; a fit of her old impetuosity seizes her; she rushes away in the darkness, takes a wrong turning, perhaps— who knows—?"

"Ah, yes; and the stream was there waiting for her, and she thought she would end it all. Poor soul!"

"Or it may be," said Loveday pityingly, "that some sweet story of sainthood and martyrdom that she had heard in her childish days came floating dimly into her brain as she made her way through the darkness, and she thought she would do her best to make atonement to the one whom she had so deeply injured by not standing in the way of his future happiness. Here is my train! Ah, yes; it is a sad, sad story!"

"Yes; for the present things are a trifle gloomy for the family at the Hall, I'll admit," said Ramsay, as he shut the carriage-door on Loveday;

CATHERINE LOUISA PIRKIS

"but they'll turn over a new leaf there before long. There'll be a couple of weddings in the house before the year comes to an end, I'll be bound."

"No," said Loveday, as she steeled herself comfortably in a corner; "Mrs. Greenhow has shown herself in her true colours at this time of distress, and, from what I hear, will stand but little chance of becoming the second Mrs. Golding. Lord Guilleroy and the runaway René are the only two who will have to be congratulated as bride and bridegroom."

A Note About the Author

Catherine Louisa Pirkis (1839–1910) was a British author known for her detective fiction. Pirkis wrote fourteen novels and contributed to many magazines and journals, sometimes publishing under her initials, C.L. Pirkis, to avoid gender discrimination. Later in her life, Pirkis transitioned away from her writing career to join her husband, Frederick Pirkis, in his fight for animals' rights. Together, the couple founded an activist organization to save animals from cruel conditions. Their organization continues their advocacy today, and now goes by the name "Dogs Trust".

A Note from the Publisher

Spanning many genres, from non-fiction essays to literature classics to children's books and lyric poetry, Mint Edition books showcase the master works of our time in a modern new package. The text is freshly typeset, is clean and easy to read, and features a new note about the author in each volume. Many books also include exclusive new introductory material. Every book boasts a striking new cover, which makes it as appropriate for collecting as it is for gift giving. Mint Edition books are only printed when a reader orders them, so natural resources are not wasted. We're proud that our books are never manufactured in excess and exist only in the exact quantity they need to be read and enjoyed.

bookfinity™

Discover more of your favorite classics with Bookfinity™.

- Track your reading with custom book lists.
- Get great book recommendations for your personalized Reader Type.
- Add reviews for your favorite books.
- AND MUCH MORE!

Visit **bookfinity.com** and take the fun Reader Type quiz to get started.

Enjoy our classic and modern companion pairings!

Classic & Modern